I Am the Only
Running Footman

I Am the Only Running Footman

MARTHA GRIMES

LITTLE, BROWN AND COMPANY
BOSTON   TORONTO

My special thanks to John Hayward of The Old Penny Palace, Brighton.

The author is grateful to the following for permission to reprint
excerpts from previously copyrighted material:

From "Stardust," Music by Hoagy Carmichael, Lyrics by
Mitchell Parrish. © 1929 Mills Music, Inc., Renewed 1957.
Copyright controlled by Mills Music, Inc. and Hoagy Publishing
Company. All rights reserved.

From "Isn't It Romantic?" by Richard Rodgers and Lorenz
Hart. Copyright © 1932 by Famous Music Corporation; Copyright © renewed 1959 by Famous Music Corporation.

To Harry Wallace
and the cat, Stripey,
the only running footmen

Sometimes I wonder why I spend
The lonely night, dreaming of a song
The melody haunts my reverie
And I am once again with you.

—"STARDUST," HOAGY CARMICHAEL,
MITCHELL PARRISH

The rain set early in to-night,
  The sullen wind was soon awake,
It tore the elm-tops down for spite,
  and did its worst to vex the lake:
I listened with heart fit to break;
  When glided in Porphyria . . .

        . . . and all her hair
  In one long yellow string I wound
Three times her little throat around,
And strangled her.

—"PORPHYRIA'S LOVER,"
ROBERT BROWNING

CONTENTS

PART I

Lonely Night

1

THE headlamps of the car picked her out through the fog and the rain; she was standing on the shoulder about a hundred yards from the cafe, her backpack on the ground beside her.

At one point, when the lorry that had been her last ride left the A30, he was afraid he might have lost her. Another one had come rattling onto a roundabout, cutting off his view. But he was fairly sure the Sainsbury lorry was heading for the motorway, on its way to Bristol or Birmingham. So he had taken the A303 exit and picked them up again.

He thought his chance had come when the driver turned into the car park of a Little Chef. But the driver and the girl both went in, so he slotted his blue Ford saloon into the short line of fog-shrouded cars and went in the cafe. Sliding into a booth in the rear, he had been able to watch her. She and the driver exchanged a few words, and then a few words with a waitress, and after that conversation stopped between them. No friendship had been struck up during all of the miles he had followed them.

She was young, twenty-five or -six, but she had a hard face made harder by the sour light of the cafe, an artificial light that seemed to glance off the red tabletops and white paper napkins and starched blouses of the uniforms. The girl did not look at her companion. Her chin rested on her fisted hand and with the other she absently curled a long strand of blond hair. The waitress set down plates of beans and eggs and chips and then came back to him. He ordered tea.

They said nothing throughout their meal, finally took their separate bills and paid the expressionless cashier.

Their leaving together told him the driver was taking her farther, so he paid his bill and went out to his car, starting the engine as the lorry pulled out.

When he saw her through the fog not far from the cafe, he assumed she must have changed her mind about the driver or the destination or both. He leaned over to open the door on the passenger's side and asked her if he could give her a lift. The Ford idled on the shoulder as she slid in, tossing her rucksack on the rear seat and returning his offer with a grunt and a nod.

She was headed for Bristol, she said, as she rooted in the shoulder bag and brought out cigarette papers and a small folded paper. No, grass. The sickish-sweet odor began to fill the car. He rolled down the window.

She asked if he minded, but with no hint of apology for lighting up or intention of putting it out. The question seemed to suffice, as far as she was concerned. When he said he wasn't used to the smell, she only shrugged and turned back to stare at the windscreen, the cigarette tight in a little clip. Then, again without asking, she switched on the car radio. Voices, music swelled, died as she ran the dial back and forth, finally settling on a station where the plummy voice of a disc jockey was bringing up an old Glenn Miller recording. That surprised him; he would have expected her to listen to rock.

For three days he had been in Exeter, watching her, following her. He had watched the house from several points across the street—news agent's, launderette, a tiny restaurant called Mr. Wong and Son. He had been careful to leave the blue Ford in a public car park; he had been less careful of himself. Once he had gone into the restaurant, a dark, boxlike place with tablecloths stained by soy sauce bottles, and ordered a meal. There wouldn't be any reason to connect him with her. And the waiter—Mr. Wong's son, perhaps—had stood staring out of the window the whole time, looking from the pallor of the unpapered walls to the pallor of the pavement. His face was a mask of indifference; he would hardly remember.

It had been careless also, going into the Little Chef, rather than just waiting in his car. The car itself he had bought, together with its plates, rather than using his own. Now, as the car swam in and out of misty pools of light thrown by headlamps coming from the other direction, he reminded himself again that there was no reason for anyone to connect him with the girl.

They drove on and she neither spoke nor dropped her eyes from the windscreen. He said to her that he'd never smoked grass and she snorted and said he must live at the bottom of the sea, then. Maybe she'd fix him one, he suggested. He'd be glad to pay her for it, just for the experience. She shrugged and said okay, that it made no odds with her just as long as he paid. It was good stuff, the best. No, she didn't bloody mind if he drove off and stopped the car to smoke. Like the Chinese waiter, she was too bored to question anything. Even too bored to be suspicious.

He pulled off the road into a thicket of trees. There would be tire tracks. He knew that casts could be made of tire tracks, which is one reason he'd bought the old Ford. As he smoked the cigarette she'd handed him, he thought, There it is again—extreme care, extreme carelessness—the rational part of his mind being overridden by some other force. The chance that anyone in the cafe would recognize him after a lapse of time was slim; that there'd be a reason to recognize him, even slimmer. Still, he wondered. Had there been a compulsion to link himself to her? To sit in the same room, eat the same food, walk the same streets? He didn't know.

She didn't even ask him why he was getting out of the car, just sat there smoking, listening to the radio. With the car door open, he could hear the scratchy recording of the old song:

> *Isn't it romantic*
> *Merely to be young, on such a night as this?*

He moved a little farther off from the car. The rain had stopped, the sky had cleared. Through the black fretwork of branches he could see a few stars, far apart. Close by was a little stream, iced over, its banks hemmed with snow.

When he heard the car door on her side opening, he wasn't surprised. Too indifferent to be suspicious of his stopping or of his leaving the car, it wasn't odd that she'd leave it too. Not that it would have made any difference whether she got out or not. Her boots squelched along the wet ground as she came up beside him. "Isn't It Romantic?" kept on playing, its question insistent in the night. She asked him if he liked the grass and he said, Yes, except he was feeling whoozy. He handed her some money, which she took without a word and shoved in the top pocket of her anorak. She wore a woollen hat and her throat was wrapped in a plaid scarf, the ends falling down her back. She was pretty in a cheap, hard way; and her manner cold as the little crusted stream.

When he looked up at the sky, he felt light-headed; there was a star, he said, falling there in the west. She said he was bloody high on grass and they argued about the star. It had really fallen, he insisted.

The distant constellations, the dead stars, the bored girl.

> *Isn't it romantic,*
> *Music in the night . . . ?*

When he reached for her scarf, she probably thought he meant to draw her to him and kiss her. He pulled quickly, forcefully. Almost soundlessly, her body slumped and fell, hitting and cracking the thin crust of ice. It was as close to a lover's tryst as they would ever come, he thought, the ends of the scarf fluttering away from his hands.

Wasn't it romantic?

In this desolate pocket of silence, a dozen members of the Devon-Cornwall constabulary stood near the body like mourners. It was nearly dawn but the stars had not faded from the sky. They had been waiting for over ten minutes for Brian Macalvie to say something.

He didn't; he stood, hands in pockets and shoving back his raincoat, looking down at the ground, at the body, at the glazed coat of the stream and then up at the stars.

A twig snapped; a bird called. No one moved. Not even the Scene of Crimes expert—in this case a woman—had ventured yet to disturb Macalvie's concentration. The assumption was that a camera's flash would disturb the aura of that part of the universe here in Devon that was the particular domain of Divisional Commander Macalvie.

They were all cold and impatient, which was safe if no one decided to act on it. Unfortunately, Sergeant Gilly Thwaite, with her wide blue eyes and rotten temper, had never responded to the Macalvie magic. She nearly stomped on the corpse in her impatience to set up her tripod. "We've been standing here for fifteen minutes. Will it disturb your *mise-en-scène*, your atmosphere, your evidence if I use my brownie?" She held up her camera.

Macalvie just kept chewing his gum. "Sure, go ahead. You've screwed it up now, anyway."

The doctor, heartened by Gilly Thwaite's approach, tried dipping his own question in acid. "Do you mind if *I* go ahead with my examination?"

Someone coughed.

The difference between Sergeant Thwaite and the doctor was that Macalvie gave his sergeant credit for knowing her job. His expression didn't change; he just chewed his gum more deliberately. "I'm holding you uρ?"

Someone sighed.

The doctor was kneeling beside the girl, unclasping his bag. "I'm not your police pathologist, just a country doctor. And a busy man."

A constable dropped his head in his hand.

"I see," said Macalvie. "And what exactly do you think you're going to look for?" Macalvie turned his head again to look up at the night sky.

The doctor looked up at him. "Look for? I assume you'd like to know how she was murdered, whether she was beaten or raped." His hands moved toward the scarf.

"Uh-huh. Don't touch that yet, okay?" Macalvie asked pleasantly.

The doctor sighed hugely. "Are we going to stay out here—?"

"—the rest of the day if I say so. She was garroted, she wasn't beaten, she wasn't raped. What else you got to tell me?"

"Not even you have X-ray vision, Mr. Macalvie." He laughed briefly. "Not even you can see through a heavy anorak and blue jeans."

Macalvie might have been debating the X-ray vision comment. "At least I can *see*. Look at her jeans."

"Rapists have been known to redress their victims, Mr. Macalvie. Some are surprisingly fastidious."

Macalvie stared at the sky. "You'd have to be a fastidious damned paperhanger to yank those jeans off, much less put them back on. They're like flypaper; the legs have zippers. She probably had to lie down and use a crowbar." He turned and nodded to the rest of the team from headquarters.

Quickly, they fell about their business—literally fell, going down on hands and knees, searching every inch of ground for prints, tracks, fibers, anything.

"Name's Sheila Broome," said a uniformed constable, who'd searched the backpack. "Lived in Exeter—"

Macalvie bent down to pick up a tiny clip, a bit of white paper adhering to the end. "Roach clip. So she was standing here, smoking grass. Or they were. Killers don't usually stand around toking with their victims. Maybe it's close to home; a boyfriend, maybe."

The constable almost pitied the boyfriend as he looked at his chief.

"Get an incidents room out here," said Macalvie, walking away from the angry white glare of the camera flash.

2

RICHARD Jury had to reach across Susan Bredon-Hunt, at the same time trying to disengage himself from the long arms that always grew more tangled and vinelike when telephones rang.

She was definitely a phone-clinger. She marched her fingers up and down his chest, drew circles round his ear, dusted his face with her lashes as if she were taking prints, and generally made clever-telephone repartee impossible.

Fortunately, no clever repartee was needed. Chief Superintendent Racer, having been routed out of his bed, was determined to bounce Jury from his. "Four rings, Jury! What the hell were you doing?"

It was just as well the question was rhetorical, since Susan Bredon-Hunt's lips were brushing across his face. He raised his hand, but it was like trying to push cobwebs away. Bits and pieces of her clung everywhere.

"—hate to disturb you," said Racer, whose sarcasm poked at him like Susan Bredon-Hunt's finger. "Could you crawl out of bed and get yourself over to Mayfair?"

Crawl out was what he had to do in order to get past Susan Bredon-Hunt. Finally, sitting on the edge of the bed, he said, "Where in Mayfair?"

"Charles Street. Berkeley Square. Hays Mews." Racer barked the names out like a BritRail conductor. "Woman's been murdered." The receiver on the other end crashed down.

Jury apologized to Susan and was into his clothes in fifteen seconds.

"Just like *that!*" She snapped her fingers. "You leave just like that!"

He was tired. "That's how people get killed, love. Just like that."

When he bent to kiss her, she turned her face away.

Jury collected his coat and car keys and left.

Police cars had converged, angling toward the curb in Charles Street and up on the pavement outside of the pub. Beneath the lamplit sign of I Am the Only Running Footman, Detective Sergeant Alfred Wiggins was writing in his notebook, asking questions of the short, plump woman who had found the body.

The whirring domed lights of the last two cars to careen up in front of the pub cast blue ribbons on the wet pavement, blue shadows across the faces of Wiggins and the woman. She had been walking her dog in the square late that night, and she and it were extremely upset, she said. The Alsatian sniffed Wiggins's feet and yawned.

Jury assured her that when she was taken to the police station she would be kept no longer than absolutely necessary, that any call she wished to make could be made, that they greatly appreciated her help, that she had done something not everyone would by calling for police. This calmed her and she was answering Wiggins's questions now. Up and down the short street and around the corner, uniformed policemen were asking their own questions of the residents of Hays Mews who had come out from their trendy little houses to stand in the drizzle. Screens had been placed at the end of the mews to keep the curious from satisfying much of their curiosity.

While the medical examiner was dictating findings to a tape recorder, Jury stood and looked at the young woman's body lying face down on the street, light hair fanned out, legs jackknifed. Wiggins had come up beside him.

"Through with that?" Jury asked of the fingerprint man and pointing to the small black purse whose strap was still hitched over her shoulder, tangling with her long scarf. The man nodded to Jury and Jury nodded to Wiggins. The M.E. looked over at Jury with annoyance. She didn't like questions crossing the comments she was tossing like a knife-thrower over her shoulder at her assistant. Jury looked at her sharp gray eyes and smiled brightly. She grunted.

"Ivy Childess," said Wiggins, holding up the identification he had taken from the dead woman's purse and which he held with a handkerchief. "Address is Ninety-two Church Street, Bayswater. That's about all, sir, besides checkbook, bank card, some change. With that little bit of money, she might just have been having a drink in the pub, wouldn't you say?" He returned the license to the purse and snapped it shut.

"Might have been," said Jury, as he waited for the M.E. to finish. He knew she hated any interference.

Having brought his handkerchief into play with the purse, Wiggins used it to blow his nose. "It's this damned wet. Know I'm coming down with something. Flat on my back I'll be." His tone was pensive.

"Ivy Childess certainly is." The rain fell, steadily and tenaciously, but the medical examiner seemed not to notice it at all. Crisis-as-usual had worn her pretty face as smooth as stone under water.

"No marks I can see except for the neck. Strangled with her own scarf. Some women never learn."

Jury smiled slightly. Dr. Phyllis Nancy had a way of examining things for sexual bias, even dead bodies. Jury wanted to tell her that such bias in police work had pretty much gone the way of all flesh, male or female. But Dr. Nancy seemed as committed to her defensiveness as she was to her job.

"When can you do the autopsy, Phyllis?"

No one called her Phyllis. That's why Jury did.

"You wait your turn, Superintendent. I've got a schedule, too."

"I know. I'd just appreciate it if maybe you'd move this nearer the top. We know how she was killed and it looks pretty routine—"

Routine was not a word Phyllis Nancy liked. And his comment was, as Jury knew it would be, an opportunity for her to give a little lecture, something she seldom got a chance to do, especially around police superintendents. "The woman's still got skin, hair, fingertips, liver, pancreas, bones, tissue. Even a heart."

"So do you, Phyllis." He smiled at her. Jury had come upon Dr. Nancy once, window-shopping on New Bond Street, standing outside Dickins and Jones, ogling the elaborate display of bridal and bridesmaids' gowns. He had waited until she'd walked on to catch her up and invite her for a drink. Phyllis Nancy would hate to have been caught mooning over the Dickins and Jones window-wedding: bride, groom, lace, flowers. He turned from her to give directions to a police inspector. The street would have to be covered inch by inch. Then he turned back to Dr. Nancy. "Whenever you can, Phyllis. Thanks."

She turned away to hide a smile. The whole thing was a little ritual. If he patronized her, man to woman, he knew she got a kick out of it. Under all of that expertise and armor was a very nice person who liked to have lunches out, go to movies, buy nice clothes. She collected her bag and her assistant, said she'd get round to the autopsy as soon as she could, got in a car, streaked away through the rain.

3

It was a well-tended terraced house on a residential street dotted with estate agents' signs and a depressing similarity of facades that was not at its best in the early morning light. Next door was one of the houses for sale, unlived in from the condition of the garden, where a small climbing rose struggled for position between clumps of weeds and rusted bicycle wheels. The porches and doorframes of several of the houses had been painted in strong, riotous colors, but the dull light returned them to anonymity again, reds and blues barely distinguishable, looking caked and dried to the color of old blood.

The Childess house had kept to a bottle-brown for the small fence and the door, which looked the color originally chosen, one more in keeping with what the street was originally intended for—a sensible lower-middle-class bastion of British sobriety.

The woman who opened the door at Jury's knock wore a flannel bathrobe the color of the trim and a piece of toweling round her head either to hide the curlers there or to ease the strain when she slept. Her look at him was as taut as the door-chain.

"Mrs. Childess?" He brought his warrant card near the inch of open space. "Could we speak to you, please?"

He had seen that look many times, confusion outstripped by fear. It astonished him sometimes, the way in which otherwise imperceptive and even dull minds could in some circumstances make a leap of certainty to the worst possible conclusion. The woman knew that he had come about the girl, but had immediately buried that knowledge.

Behind her a voice full of sleep said, "Who is it, Irene?"

Into that uncertain silence between the question put by the thin-faced husband and her reply to it, Jury dropped his request to come in. The door closed and the latch scraped back.

As they entered, Wiggins touched his fingers to his hat. That part of Jury's mind that permitted escape into minutiae reminded him to buy a hat; he hated hats. He introduced himself and his sergeant to the couple, and the man, whom she had addressed as Trevor, blinked and started apologizing for the lapsed road tax sticker.

"It's not about that, Mr. Childess. I'm afraid that something's happened to your daughter. She was found in Berkeley Square. She was dead." There was no way to prepare anyone for this, no way to soften the blow; Jury had always felt stretching it out with words like "accident" only added to the agony. If you saw the crash was inevitable, if the lorry was bearing down on you, you shouldn't have to stare at the headlamps too long. "I'm terribly sorry."

Neither the mother nor the father said, *That's impossible*, or *That couldn't have happened*, or otherwise tried to hold the knowledge at bay. Maybe it was the heavy note of finality in his voice; maybe it was the empathy. Mrs. Childess's veined hands flew to her mouth, and she shook her head, tears spattering like rain. Her husband stared; his arm came up automatically to fall across her shoulders.

When finally they had sat down in a small parlor too full of Ivy Childess for much comfort, Jury waited for a few moments while she tried to combat another rush of tears. Wiggins, who always had a fresh supply of handkerchiefs somewhere about him, pushed one into her hands. Jury asked a few routine questions about Ivy in as dry a tone as possible without being curt. Too much sympathy was often worse than none at all. When the father finally asked what had happened and where, Jury put it as briefly and kindly as possible. "There didn't seem to have been much of a struggle and she must have died very quickly."

"But who could possibly have wanted to—do that to our Ivy?" Mrs. Childess said, addressing her husband as if he might have some secret store of knowledge about Ivy. "I don't understand. I just don't understand." She leaned her face against her husband's thin chest.

"That's why we're here, Mrs. Childess; that's what we want to find out. If you could bear with us a bit . . ." He nodded to Wiggins, who sat back and opened his notebook. "Could you tell us anything about her friends? Men, especially."

Trevor Childess looked startled. "Well, yes. There was one named Marr. Ivy said as how she was kind of engaged to him. Marr. Yes, I'm sure that's the name, wasn't it, Irene? David Marr, she said. Bit of a catch that was—" And he smiled briefly before he realized that the catch would never be landed.

"How long had your daughter known him?"

The question seemed to make Childess uncomfortable; he shifted in his chair and studied his hands when he answered. "Well, we didn't really know him, I suppose." That apparently sounded very odd even to his own ears, and he looked at the drawn face of his wife for direction.

Jury didn't think she'd heard her husband. The flow of tears had stopped, but the handkerchief was still wadded against her mouth and her arm was across her stomach, holding herself like something broken.

"Never did get round to coming here," said the father, "though Ivy kept saying she'd bring him to tea one day."

The father glanced quickly around the room and Jury saw what he saw: a parlor, well tended like the yard, neat and orderly, but plain if not actually shabby. The suite of furniture, probably purchased on hire-purchase, armchairs and a sofa covered with an afghan probably crocheted by his wife or a relative in colors that should brighten the place but only increased its anonymity.

To avoid heaping even more distress on the man's platter—inconsequential but still humiliating—Jury offered him a cigarette, lit one himself, and got up to walk about the parlor. He nodded to Wiggins to continue the questioning.

Several of his colleagues at headquarters had asked Jury why, given his position, he did not avail himself of a detective inspector for an assistant. Jury asked them why he should, told them the sergeant had saved his life at least twice. That was the truth, but it wasn't the reason. Jury respected Wiggins, for Wiggins felt a strong bond with those who were often labeled as underdogs. Sergeant Wiggins's presence was soothing; he gave witnesses the impression somehow that he was one of them, had come amongst them with his notebook and pen; his economical, even parsimonious gestures; his long silences and sympathetic stares (often not related to the problem at hand); not to mention his roster of maledictions that nudged awake the sleeping hypochondria in everyone; his ability to scale the Metropolitan Police down to the pleasant bobby on the corner. In an old morality play, Wiggins would have been the shepherd come to bear witness. And he always had a spare handkerchief.

Which he was using now, blowing his nose in the cold, dawn-lit parlor, along with Mrs. Childess, whose most recent bout with tears appeared to be, at least temporarily, under control. She held the handkerchief wadded in her lap; Wiggins stuffed his back in his pocket and went on with his routine questions in his nice, monotonous voice.

Given the photographs on the mantel, it seemed that Ivy had been the only child. Several snapshots were set round two studio portraits; one of the portraits was probably taken when she was eighteen or nineteen, a full-length photo in which she was holding a few drooping roses. The end of school term, perhaps, or of childhood. Her expression was rather smug and knowing, as if she'd passed through a bothersome phase of her life. The second might have been taken yesterday. Her hair spread like clear water over the shoulders of a jumper that he recognized as the one she'd been wearing when she was murdered, blue, scoop-necked, full-sleeved. He returned the photo to its place on the mantel and picked up its mate—a small one, unframed, also recent. Jury went back to the others and sat down a short distance away so that Wiggins could continue.

The mother looked completely spent; she rested her head, eyes closed, against the button-tufted back of the chair. The father had been talking about his daughter's job at Boots. "Makeup consultant, she was."

For this, Jury read sales assistant.

"Did you know any of her other friends, aside from what you'd heard of the fiancé?"

Again, Trevor Childess looked a little shamefaced as he shook his head. "Ivy never did go out much when she lived with us. She wasn't one for pubs and the like. She was more a homebody, like her mother."

There was a silence, during which Mrs. Childess roused herself and left the room. Then Jury rose and Wiggins pocketed his notebook. He told Childess he would have to be called on to identify his daughter's body. The man's face was blank and ashen.

"I'm sorry, Mr. Childess. It has to be you or your wife and I wanted to wait until she was safely tucked in before even bringing it up." Jury knew that the appeal to a greater strength than his wife could call on would help to give the man some purpose. "It can wait, at least until later today. We'll send a car round."

Childess murmured something that might have been unfelt thanks and then said to Wiggins, "You won't be coming yourself, then?"

"Sorry, sir. We'll be getting on immediately to whoever might have been with Ivy." From his coat pocket he pulled the packet of lozenges. "You don't want to let that cough go. Take these."

Whatever it was—amulet or anodyne—Trevor Childess took the packet gratefully.

"Terrible thing," said Wiggins, slamming the door shut on the driver's side. "And Ivy being the only one." Wiggins always got on a first-name basis with the victims quickly. It was part of his charm.

"Yes. Only, I wonder. If there were five or six or ten, would it be much comfort? If you lose one, don't you suppose it's like losing them all?"

The engine turned over, coughed asthmatically, and went dead. Wiggins tried again, mumbling. Death and weather had a way of knitting themselves together in his mind. "You'd think they'd give us something better than this ten-year-old Cortina," he said darkly as he tried to nurse the engine and hit the heater into action.

"What about Marr?"

"David L. Ex-directory and I thought for a moment I was going to have to call headquarters to get the address. Bloody operator gave it to me finally." The engine turned over and he pulled away from the curb. "It's Mayfair, all right. I didn't call him; didn't think you'd want to alert him."

"Good. Where in Mayfair?"

"Shepherd Market." He took his hands from the steering wheel and blew on them. "Not far from the Running Footman, is it?"

"No. Walking, how long?"

Wiggins thought for a moment. "Ten minutes, maybe. But I don't suppose he'd be walking in all this muck."

Despite the errand and the cold, Jury smiled. The new snow furred the rusted car parts and rimmed the garishly painted porches and woodwork, blanketed the shabbiness of the street ahead. It lay blue and untrammeled in the morning light. Undisturbed, it seemed to bond the houses and fences together.

4

D AVID Marr fit his surroundings. He looked elegant and neglected. The knap of his dressing gown was as badly rubbed as the Axminster carpet, and the cord as frayed as the tasseled one that held back the Chinese silk curtain. The one on the robe hung at approximately the same angle as Marr's head. At six A.M. he was probably in the grip of a whale of a hangover.

Hangover or not, the man was handsome. Jury thought there was something vaguely familiar about the high cheekbones and dark hair, or perhaps it was the sort of face that might have belonged to some dissolute peer, one often served up by the seamier tabloids along with sex, drugs and girls.

Right now David Marr was sprawled in a worn-leather wing chair. His first reaction to the murder of Ivy Childess had been bafflement more than grief. His second, third, and fourth, Jury had been unable to see, since a cold flannel completely covered Marr's face, and had done during Jury's questions so far. Probably he could have used one or the other of Sergeant Wiggins's remedies, but Jury had sent Wiggins to the Bayswater flat.

"Go on, then." The muffled voice came from under the cloth.

"Mr. Marr, do you think perhaps we can talk face-to-face? It would be a help."

Sighing, he said, "So you can see the subtle change of expression that will testify to my guilt?" His breath sucked in and puffed out the cloth that he now withdrew reluctantly. "It's not that I drank so much, it's that I stupidly drank the Dogbolter at the Ferret and Firkin. Bruce's Brewery, my friend. I was doing a bit of a pub-crawl before I met Ivy." He dropped the flannel on a small table, and took the last cigarette from a black enamel case. "I'm being an insensitive boor, right?"

Jury smiled. "If you say so. You think I'm presuming you're guilty?"
Jury lit up one of his own cigarettes.

Marr looked at Jury with a grim smile. "Your questions suggest that
you've ruled out the most obvious answer: that poor Ivy was set upon by
some mugger." He looked away, toward the window where the pre-dawn
darkness was as black as the enamel on the lighter he fingered. "Was she
raped?"

"I don't know yet." Jury pictured the body, a pale blue heap in the
middle of the wet street. "I don't think so. Would you mind telling me
what happened at the pub?"

Marr scrubbed at his hair with the cloth, then studied the end of his
cigarette with an indifference that Jury suspected was feigned.

"We had an argument. She was angry and refused to let me take her
home to Bayswater." He looked at Jury. "I don't usually leave women
standing in pub doorways." He shrugged. "Ivy can be extremely stubborn.
Doesn't look it, really, all that soft blue look and gorgeous hair. Well, I
don't really care for confrontations with women. Not worth it."

"What was the argument about, Mr. Marr?"

"Money, marriage, you know. For some reason Ivy wanted to marry
me, poor girl."

"I'd think one reason might be pretty obvious—you move in a much
headier social circle, I imagine."

David Marr opened one eye. "How can you tell that?"

The question was rather innocent. Jury smiled. "I've been to the
Childess house."

"Bayswater?"

"Mile End. The parents' house. They were the ones who gave me your
name."

He frowned. "She hardly ever spoke of them. Hadn't much family feeling, had Ivy."

"But you *were* engaged."

Marr paused, his eyes shielded by his hand, in lookout fashion, as if he
were tracking the progress of the morning light at the window. "That what
the parents told you?"

"That's what the daughter told *them.*"

The hand now pressed to his head, as if he were holding it on, Marr
pushed himself out of the wing chair and moved toward a rosewood table.
He held a bottle of Remy to his ear like a huge shell, shook it and put it
down, frowning. Then he studied the remaining inch or two in a Glenfiddich bottle, looked over at Jury, and held it up by way of not very enthusi-
astic invitation.

"Too early for me, thanks, or too late, depending how you look at it."

Marr poured the inch and a half into a tumbler. "I try not to look at it at all. If you're going to swallow a frog, better not stare at it too long, as they say. My head is killing me." He drank it down and retied the robe. "A boor I may be—desolute, depraved, whatever. But engaged I was not. Whether that particular bit of information is important to your investigations, I don't know; you've only my word for it. Whatever she told friends, family, co-workers, I didn't mean to marry Ivy." He fell into the chair again and relit his cigarette.

"What was your relationship with her?"

"Um. Intimate, or at least sexual. There's probably a difference."

Jury was mildly surprised he'd make the distinction. Marr looked quite human with some of the cool hauteur missing from his voice and eyes. "Then the 'engagement' was a fiction invented by her?" Marr nodded. "Then she was simply trying to convince herself?"

"Trying to convince *me* is more like it." He closed his eyes and shook his head slightly. "On several occasions she definitely talked of marriage. Such as last night."

"What did you say?"

"I didn't answer. Have another fag on you, Superintendent?"

Jury handed him the packet and leaned back. "Are you sure you did nothing to encourage her?"

Marr eased himself down in the chair, crossed his long legs, and shook his head in wonder. "For heaven's sakes. A few nights in bed over a period of several months would hardly give anyone but the most naïve of women *that* sort of encouragement, would it? I did not absolutely say, No, we are not going to be married, but I do think I showed a certain amount of hesitancy over it. . . ."

"You left the pub around closing time?"

"About ten-forty-five or -fifty. When last drinks were called."

"Did Ivy stay on or did she leave?"

"The last I saw of her she was standing in the doorway, hand on hip, coat collar pulled up, looking extremely determined." He sighed and rubbed his head again. "Shouldn't have had the last of the Remy, I expect. She told me to more or less bugger off and I did. That's the last I saw of her, Superintendent."

"The Running Footman would have closed shortly after that. She'd have taken a cab to her flat in Bayswater, wouldn't she?"

Marr smiled ruefully. "Knowing Ivy, she might have taken the underground. Cheaper."

"You came directly home?"

Marr sighed. "Yes, of course. It's only a few minutes' walk. When I got here I called my sister, Marion. Talked for some time, but to no avail. I needed money."

"You said money was one of the things you quarreled with Ivy Childess about."

"That's right. I tried to borrow some."

"But surely Ivy Childess wouldn't have had the sort you might need."

Marr laughed. "If it has Her Majesty's face on it, I need it. The odd tailor here and there. A few gambling debts. Ivy would not dip into the money from her uncle's annuity; told me I should be gainfully employed. Yes, that's the way she put it: gainfully employed. I have *never* been employed. Much less gainfully. Work, good Lord."

"Yes, that does seem a dim future."

"That sort of irony exactly matches my sister's. She tells me I'm running through my share of our father's money with a speed that would have earned me a rowing Blue. Our solicitors do not like to advance me more than a sum which would hardly pay for the liquor." This reminder of drink sent him back to the table laden with bottles, where he found a measure or two of whiskey and poured it out.

Jury made another note in a worn pigskin notebook that Racer had in one of his rare moments of largess given him several Christmases ago. Or perhaps it wasn't largess, just a hint to get to work. "You said you called your sister. Could you give me her number?"

"You're not going to bother old Marion with this, are you? Oh, very well." He raked his fingers through his hair, sighed, and gave Jury the number. "It's ex-directory, so don't lose it." His smile came and vanished in a second. "She's not going to be happy about corroborating my alibi, if that's what you call it."

"You said 'after you got home'? Exactly when after?"

"After the rest of this, I suppose." He held up the glass and turned it so that the whiskey ran round it in a little wave.

"Could you be more exact?" Jury asked mildly, quite sure that the man's offensive carelessness over the girl's death was pretty much facade. Underneath it, he was frightened, but how much, Jury couldn't guess.

He closed his eyes. "A little after eleven, perhaps. Don't hold it to me, Superintendent. Marion would know. She was sober. Always is, worse luck. Her name is Winslow and they have a place in Sussex, in Somers Abbas. Look, Superintendent. Couldn't you just leave old Marion out of this?"

"You want me to be discreet, that it?"

The clear, wide-eyed look on his handsome face made Marr look as if he'd just come wandering in from larking with a bag of kittens down at the lake. Wonderfully innocent and sly. "Oh, would you? I'd cooperate all over the place. You can question me for hours—"

"I would do, anyway."

"You're not going to cooperate, I can tell. I have reservations for Tuesday next for Cannes, but I expect I shan't be permitted to leave the country now. Cigarette?" He looked at Jury's.

Jury tossed him the pack. "My guess is you called Mrs. Winslow because you were anxious to pay your tailor and she couldn't see eye-to-eye, that right?"

"Clever of you. Well, I was dead drunk, wasn't I?"

"Oh?"

Marr looked at him through the small spiral of smoke. " 'Oh?' What's that supposed to mean? You're worse than Marion."

"Nothing."

"I'll bet. Well, there's plenty of money. Although I curse the arrangement at least once a day, I suppose our father was smarter than I like to give him credit for, not putting it up for grabs. The bulk of my own inheritance is contingent upon my marrying." He sounded rueful, then added, "Am I giving myself a motive for murder?"

"The opposite, I'd say."

"Good; let's keep it that way. As it is, I can only dip into the family treasure chest four times a year. This quarter's not up until December thirty-first, worse luck." He looked at a calendar attached to a bulletin board above a handsome lacquered desk. Jury could see that it held photos, cards, other bits and pieces of memorabilia. "Mind if I have a look?"

"Hm? Oh, no, of course not. I'll just have a lie-down." His head fell back on the chair and he rolled his whiskey glass across his brow.

The bulletin board was, Jury saw with a smile, more like the carefully chosen junk of an undergraduate, or the sort of lot one might expect to find in a youngster's shoebox of treasures: photos, of course; colorful and witless postcards such as people loved to send from their holiday spots in the West Country, or the Riviera, Monte Carlo, Las Vegas, Cannes.

"Been to the States?"

David looked round to the bulletin board. "No."

"You have friends there, then?" He nodded toward the card of a Vegas casino.

"No. An acquaintance or two. My *friends* go to Monte or Cannes, Superintendent."

Jury smiled. "Sorry. Didn't know there was much to choose amongst them." He continued scanning the board. A menu from Rules, a silver garter, telephone numbers on scraps of paper tacked about. Jury was more interested in the snapshots. "Is this your sister?"

With a wince, David turned his head. "Yes, and the rest of the family. That's my nephew and my sister's husband, Hugh."

It had been taken in a garden; they all looked very pleased with themselves, as if they were delighted to have met and had their picture taken.

Another snap showed David Marr with the same young man, both of them laughing, holding what looked like tennis racquets. There were no photos of Marr by himself, none with Ivy Childess.

"Would you mind if I just borrowed these two?"

David was about to cadge another cigarette from Jury's pack. "What? No, I don't mind, I suppose. Just make sure I get them back, that's all."

"I will."

"What do you want them—? Oh, never mind. To show round, I expect. You're probably convinced I dragged Ivy into a dark street and—what *did* happen, Superintendent?"

"That's what we're trying to find out. Was there anyone else in the pub you knew?"

He started to shake his head, but then said, "Yes, there was Paul. Paul Swann. He lives down the street. If he hadn't been in the Running Footman, I'd have stopped in to talk to him, worse luck."

"Perhaps I'll stop in to talk to him."

"Can't. He's not there. Said he was leaving for Brighton at dawn."

"Where in Brighton?"

David scratched his head. "Don't know. Maybe it's Rottingdean. That's more artistic; he's a painter."

Jury made a note, and said, "Then as far as you know, Miss Childess simply left when the pub closed. Did you have any friends in common? Acquaintances?"

He frowned and slid down in the chair. "No."

"You knew of no one she considered an enemy?"

David Marr shook his head and picked up the flannel. He dipped it in what remained of his drink and slapped it on his forehead.

"You know, you seem more irritated by Ivy Childess's death than unhappy." Jury rose to leave.

The flannel moved as David Marr said, "Good God, Superintendent, I'm not irritated. I'm dying." He pulled the cloth from his face, gave Jury a weak smile and asked, "Got another fag?"

5

❧ ~ ❧

IONA Clingmore sat at her desk with a mirror propped up against a
dictionary, applying her eyeliner with the solemnity of one taking
the veil. The hand that held the thin wand of lipstick was steadied
by the other, and the prayerful pose further enhanced the similarity. That
prayerful pose and the black scarf holding back her heavy yellow curls
were about as close as Fiona would ever get to a nunnery.

Watching over her small arsenal of beauty products was the cat Cyril,
who never seemed to tire of tracking the daily metamorphosis, as if expecting a butterfly to emerge from this black cocoon.

Cyril took his cue from Jury's entrance and slid from the desk. The cat
knew by now that this foreshadowed admittance to Racer's office—hal-
lowed ground, strictly off cat-limits.

"Hullo, Fiona," said Jury.

Realizing that Jury was standing there smiling, she deposited the tissue
on which she had blotted her lips in the dustbin. Then she quickly pulled
the black square from her head and a neat set of yellow curls sprang forth.
Just as deftly, she swept the makeup into the black well of her purse.
Permed and polished, she turned to Jury.

"You're early. Want some tea?"

"Thanks. Did you get that file from forensics?"

"Mmm." With the hot water pot in one hand and a chipped cup in the
other, she nodded toward her desk. She swirled the teabag and handed
Jury the cup.

"What's he on about, then?" asked Jury, long used to conferences with
his superior that left him feeling older but none the wiser.

"I don't know, do I?" It was less a shrugging off of Jury's question than
an indication that their superior was seldom on about anything that either
wanted to know. Having inspected a fingernail, she got her manicure scis-

sors. Fiona went at any imperfection quickly and summarily; she reminded Jury of a water-colorist alert to sudden shifts in shade and lighting who had to move in before the paint dried.

"I'll wait inside." Jury took his tea and the file and, accompanied by the cat Cyril, went into his chief's office, which Fiona apparently was "airing out" again, for the window behind the desk was open a few inches. Between his hand-rolled cigars and his hand-grown lectures, Racer managed to use up all the excess oxygen. Cyril leapt to the sill and flattened himself so that he could make swipes at the falling snowflakes.

Jury looked without interest round the office. Nothing had changed except that a small mountain of Christmas gifts was piled up on the fake-leather couch. Jury took out a fresh pack of Players. Cyril, who had managed to squeeze all the way out to the outside sill, tired of his daredevil acrobatics, pulled himself back, and made a perfect high-dive for the floor. His flirtation with death grew bolder every year; when the outside door opened, he pricked up his ears, snaked across the carpet, and settled down with a rustle behind the pyramid of gifts on the couch.

Chief Superintendent A. E. Racer made his usual abrasive comments to Fiona Clingmore before he came in to look suspiciously at the pile of gifts, as if Jury might have nicked one in his absence.

"Happy Christmas," said Jury pleasantly, as Racer deposited several folders on his desk and sat down.

"Not for me it isn't," he said, waving his arm across the active files he was carrying. Action, Jury knew, would be taken elsewhere. "What progress have you made on this Childess case?" Without stopping for an answer, Racer said, "Couldn't you shut up the press, at least?"

"Can anyone? I made no comment."

"With this rag you don't have to." He waved a tabloid in Jury's face and then read: " 'Garroted with her own scarf.' Hell. Every villain in London —rapists, muggers—will have a nice, neat way to go about his business."

"Well, it might warn women not to toss their scarves down their backs."

"A bit late in the day for that, isn't it?"

As if Jury had failed to issue the warning, had alerted the papers.

Racer crossed his arms, encased in what looked like cashmere from his bespoke tailor, and leaned toward Jury. "As for you, Jury—"

It was ritual, like Cyril's storming of the battlements. *As for you—*

"—do you think *this* time you could depend on police for your backup? Rather than deputizing your friends?" For Racer, Melrose Plant's role in that Hampshire business was a brand-new drum to bang. "Do you realize I'm still catching flack from the commissioner about *that?*"

"He did save my life."

Finding nothing here that merited a response, Racer went on to test the waters of Jury's career, keeping as much as he could to the shallows. The career had probably come up in Racer's meeting with the assistant commissioner and would be bobbing up again, as it was now. "Understand Hodges is retiring. Picked a fine time for it, I must say."

There would be for Racer, of course, some personal affront to the lawkeeping forces of Greater London in what he seemed to think was Divisional Commander Hodges's capricious decision. That it left a district minus one of its divisional commanders was a point that Racer would sooner skirt around. For Racer it would be a real quandary if Jury were promoted. Having Jury around was like having a mirror in which a face formed out of smoke reminding Racer that someone fairer still lived; on the other hand, the removal of Jury was the removal of Jury's expertise, which now reflected happily upon Racer.

He was still talking about N Division. "Wouldn't have it on a bet, myself, not with its spilling over into Brixton. Riots, that's what anyone can expect with that thankless job." He went on. . . .

Jury tuned him out, turning his attention to the pyramid of gifts that had shifted slightly, and wondered, with a momentary pang of envy, at Cyril's determination to outwit the forces leveled against him. Racer was descending the ladder of Jury's career and would soon move from the CID to the uniform branch and have Jury back walking a beat. Jury, though, was way ahead of, or way behind him, in that sense. He wondered, with a feeling of guilt, at his own lack of ambition. He had nearly had to be shoved into a superintendency as it was. Perhaps it was the season; Christmas had never been any reason for rejoicing, except for one or two that might have started well, but ended miserably. Or perhaps it was the sky. Jury watched the snow drift down in big, feathery flakes that wouldn't stick, that would turn to gray slush by nightfall and drain away. He remembered the two boys, fourteen or fifteen they'd been, that he'd nicked twenty years ago for shoplifting in a sweet shop. They'd looked very pale and uncertain and reminded him of himself a dozen years earlier, younger even than they, when the owner of a similar shop had caught him leaving the store with a small box of Black Magic chocolates making a bulge in his anorak. He'd been easier on the teenagers than the shopkeeper had been on him, the way he'd called in police. *Set an example.* The aunt who'd just taken Richard in had been mortified.

The girl's name had been Ivy, he suddenly recalled. It was Ivy he'd wanted to give the sweets to as a Christmas present. But this sentiment hadn't softened the set of his aunt's mouth. His uncle had been a gentle man, one who made allowances, especially for a nephew whose own parents had been killed in the war. But his uncle's disappointment, the woeful look he cast upon the boy Richard, had been more difficult to bear than a physical blow.

Well, it wasn't nicking sweets anymore, he thought with an almost overwhelming remorse, as the pale face of the pretty girl lying in the street came back to him. Ivy. The name was probably the reason that memory had floated to mind.

". . . Jury! Can you stop woolgathering long enough to answer the question?"

"Sorry."

"I asked you if Phyllis Nancy had done the autopsy."

"No, not yet. Tomorrow morning."

"What the hell's she waiting for, her medical degree?" Racer slapped open the top folder once again. "So all we know about this Childess woman is that she lived in Bayswater, had a row with her boyfriend in this pub off Berkeley Square, and that he left her there." He shut the folder and leaned back. "You knew all that last night, Jury."

"Then perhaps I'd better be getting on with it? Anything else?" He unfolded himself from the chair and got up, casting his eye toward the couch.

"Well, when you *do* turn up something, lad, would you kindly let me know?"

"Be happy to." Jury eyed the small tower of gifts and turned to go. When he reached the door he heard it—them: the collapse of the boxes like a house of cards, the spillage, the voice of Racer shouting at the cat Cyril, the intercom and the voice of Racer shouting at Fiona.

Calmly, Jury opened the door and Cyril streaked through before him, another game-plan successfully executed.

"He's in a right temper now," said Fiona, filing her nails, undisturbed by the squawking intercom. Cyril had leapt to the windowsill behind her to have a wash as the telephone rang.

Fiona picked it up, spoke, then held it toward Jury. The black receiver looked like an extension of her darkly varnished nails. It fairly dripped from her hand. "It's Al."

Jury took the receiver, wondering if anyone else at headquarters besides Fiona called Detective Sergeant Wiggins by his first name. "Wiggins?"

The voice of Wiggins was adenoidal, but precise. "I've come up with something, sir. I was just checking in the computer room—" The pause then was not for dramatic effect but to allow the sergeant to rustle a bit of cellophane from a box. He apparently had completed his delicate maneuver, for now the voice was clotted. " 'N du-v'n'n, s'r—"

"Shove the cough drop under your tongue, Wiggins," said Jury patiently.

"Oh. Sorry, sir. It was this case about ten months ago, end of February. Young woman by the name of Sheila Broome. Well, I would have passed straight over it except for the description of the body *in situ*. Police made sure there was no publicity because they were afraid of copy-cat murders. For good reason. She was found in a wooded area off the A303, just near the turn-off to Taunton. She'd been strangled, apparently with her own scarf. Well, it could be a coincidence—"

Jury stared blindly at Cyril, who was pressing one paw and then the other against the big snowflakes drifting against the windowpane. A serial killer. The worst kind. "Let's hope so. Get on to headquarters in Somerset."

"Police in Somerset wouldn't be handling it, sir. It's right over the border." Pause. "In Devon."

"Well, call Exeter, then."

There was another pause and a tiny rattle of paper. This seemed to be a two-cough-drop problem. Said Wiggins, wanly: "You don't suppose it's Macalvie's case, do you, sir?"

Jury half-smiled. "Every case in Devon is Macalvie's case."

6

THE snow outside the Jack and Hammer was tracked only by a narrow set of marks made by the Jack Russell belonging to Miss Crisp, which had left its mistress's rag-and-bone shop across the street to make its afternoon rounds of the village.

Through the dreamy motley of palette-tinted shops and cottages the sonorous drone of the bell in the church tower washed over the High Street and past the pub where the mechanical smith up on a high beam picked it up and made a simulated bong on his forge. Above him the clock struck five.

It was a call-to-arms for a few of Long Piddleton's residents. There was a half-hour yet until opening, but Scroggs often turned a blind eye to the licensing laws when it came to his family of regulars. One of these had biked the half-mile from Ardry End and was sitting at a table in the large bay window. His legs were outstretched and his trousers still pinched by bicycle clips. He had passed the halfway mark in the book he was reading.

No devotee of the thriller-novel, he would have ordinarily skipped from the first chapter to the last, filling in whatever extraneous details were necessary for the resolution. But his longstanding affection for the author of this particular book had obligated him to read every page. Well, almost, thought Melrose Plant. Love me, love my books. His friendship with its author had not extended to a friendship with this book bearing the irrelevant title of *The Plum-Pudding Group*. It was meant, he imagined, to sell to the Christmas trade and had found its way onto the shelves of Long Piddleton's new book shop, called the Wrenn's Nest, a silly pun on its proprietor's name.

He wondered if he couldn't just take a peek at the end. The murderer's motive was the old kill-him-before-he-changes-his-will cliché, and the characters seemed at a loss to know what to do with themselves, like people looking vague on a railway platform after the train pulls away.

Melrose Plant checked his watch, not to see if the two others who usually joined him in the Jack and Hammer were late, but because he knew another body should be turning up—ah, yes, there it was. Colonel Montague. Too bad, he thought. He had rather liked old Montague despite that gin-beneath-the-palms manner that the author had saddled him with. Yes, there were bodies aplenty. If Raymond Chandler's prescription for a cure for midbook boredom was to bring in a man with a gun, Polly Praed's was to drag another corpse into every other chapter. This latest book must have been written in extreme agitation, for there was a jittery, hectic quality to the sudden discovery of body after body. Her mind, he thought, must be an abattoir.

All this murder and mayhem was interrupted by the arrival of two other regulars whom he was happy to see since they would relieve him of further delving into the death of Montague.

"Hello, Melrose," said Vivian Rivington, the prettier of the two, although Melrose wondered idly if Marshall Trueblood would insist upon a reevaluation of that assessment.

"Hullo, old bean," said Marshall Trueblood, looking this afternoon like a fairly ordinary rather than an eccentric millionaire. He wore a dark woolen jacket so beautifully tailored that it might have been the last best dream of a Hebredean weaver. But the weaver would have wakened wide-eyed at sight of the bold blue cashmere sweater and sea green ascot tucked in the neck of a turquoise crepe de chine shirt. For Trueblood, this was a costume downplayed. "Thank God, another day in the stews and sweats is finished."

Marshall Trueblood could afford anything but sweat. He was fond of slandering his own antiques business located in the small Tudor building next door, a thriving shop despite Long Piddleton's slender population. It prospered because it drew on a London clientele, among them some very knowledgeable dealers. Business was also helped along by the patronage of the two—even richer than Trueblood—who shared the table.

"It's only just gone five," said Vivian Rivington with a melancholy air. Winter's dregs left the trio with little to do but comment on one another's departure from the norm. "You don't close until six," she said, shaking her watch.

"There's no custom. I left a sign on the door to check over here if someone wants a distressed bureau. What're you reading, Melrose?" he asked as Scroggs set drinks before them.

Melrose Plant turned it cover-out so that his friends could see.

"The Plum-Pudding Group. Strange title. Cheers." He raised his glass.

Vivian was squinting at the name of the author. "It's another one of that Polly's, isn't it?"

"I'm afraid it's not very good. But don't tell her."

"She's not *around* to tell," said Vivian with just a touch of fractiousness. "I don't understand what your relationship is."

"Careful, careful, Vivian. You're not one to talk of *engagé* involvements."

"You're so right, Melrose," said Trueblood. "Is this another Christmas you'll not be spending with the ill-starred Franco of Florence?"

"Venice," she said, a little waspishly.

"Did you get bad news in your letter?" Trueblood dashed a bit of ash from the end of his black Sobranie and smiled roguishly.

Vivian's eyes narrowed. "What do you mean, in my letter?"

"Why, the one you must have got this morning. The one in your pocket."

The hand that had strayed to the pocket of her cardigan was brought back quickly to make a fist on the table.

"Postmarked Venezio."

"Just how do *you* know?"

"If Miss Quarrels *must* sort the post by spreading it out on the counter like a cardsharp, is it my fault?"

"And you went to the trouble of reading it upside-down!"

He had brought out his little gold nail-clipper. "No, I turned it rightside up."

"Snoop!"

Hearing her cue, Lady Agatha Ardry appeared in the Jack and Hammer's doorway, making her snowy entrance with a shake-out of her cape and a stamp of her shoes. "I looked in your windows, Mr. Trueblood," she said to Marshall Trueblood even before she called to Dick Scroggs for her double shooting sherry. "It's not six, Mr. Trueblood. Your shop should be open. But then if custom means so little . . . my dear Plant, I was just bucketing along to Ardry End—"

Doing her rounds like Miss Crisp's terrier, thought Melrose, turning a page and finding Lady Dasher dead in the hydrangeas. . . .

"—and I passed a car—"

Lucky for the driver. Usually she just drove into them. Agatha had acquired an old Morris Minor that looked like her: rounded dome and dumpy body.

"—just coming down the drive as I drove in. Woman driver, thirtyish, brown hair, black Porsche—"

"Number plate?"

"What?"

"Surely, you got the number so we can run it through Scotland Yard's computer system. They do wonders finding hot cars these days—"

"Don't be daft, Plant. Well, she got straight away before I could stop her. Who is she, then? She's *not* terribly attractive."

This was said with some relief, as if removing the lady in the Porsche from the running of marriageable females. These Agatha appeared to see as so many lovelies hastening toward the family vaults of Ardry End, its chinoiserie, crystal, Queen Anne furniture, and the titles that Melrose had dropped like petals in the dust—earldom, viscountcy, baronetcy—that could still be gathered up (she seemed to think) and glued back on the bud.

"You don't have visitors this time of year, Melrose." She sighed and called again for her sherry. Scroggs went on turning the pages of his newspaper. "It's not like the old days. Remember your dear mother, Lady Marjorie—"

Here she would go again, poking along the paths of his family memories like a pig rooting through rosebushes. "The Countess of Caverness, yes. And my father, and my uncle Robert. I have always had a very good memory for detail. But what were you doing up at Ardry End?"

"To see Martha about the Christmas dinner. She said it hadn't been decided yet."

"It has. Poor Man's Goose and Idiot Biscuits."

"My favorite!" said Marshall Trueblood. "I hope we're invited."

"Of course. You always are."

"You're making it up," said Agatha, stomping her cane on the floor in an attempt to unglue Scroggs from his paper. "There's no such thing."

"There certainly is. It's actually ox-liver. And for your sweet you may have raspberry flummery. Or would you prefer the gooseberry fool? Martha's quite good with a fool." Melrose yawned and watched the Jack Russell through the leaded window that spelled out Hardy's Crown in amber lettering. It was sniffing round the feet of a woman in a brown hat standing on the pavement looking speculatively at Trueblood's window. Melrose thought she looked familiar.

"There she is!" cried Agatha, craning her neck to peer through the leaded glass.

"I didn't mean to barge in," said the young woman in the brown hat.

It was, thought Melrose, looking at the dreamy, gawky girl, exactly the sort of comment that Lucinda St. Clair would make. She was the sort of woman who people would still refer to as a "girl" even in her late twenties or early thirties.

"You're not barging!" said Vivian with the first display of brightness she had shown since she'd walked in.

For Melrose, Vivian Rivington had always embodied in near-equal measure beauty, grace, and kindliness. She could wear as she now did the old wool skirt and twinset or doll herself up in what Trueblood designated as "the Italian period," but she still never seemed to know what to do with herself or whether the one or the other persona fit. Thus it wasn't surprising that she should take the measure of Lucinda St. Clair, probably thinking that here was a female in even worse shape than she, Vivian; one who was dressed in an even drabber twinset.

"Thank you very much," said Lucinda with a look of gratitude hardly occasioned by the simple act of Trueblood's pulling out a chair for her. He himself knew Sybil St. Clair, her mother, who was an occasional customer of his. This made it that much worse for Agatha—that even Trueblood had indirect knowledge of their visitor and she none.

Lucinda's eyes were large and chestnut brown. When they met the beady black ones of Agatha, she quickly looked away. Agatha had been silently scouring Lucinda St. Clair for signs of marriageability, signs which Agatha always seemed to think such ladies sported in neon-bright arrows. Then Agatha squinted and demanded to know if they had met.

Melrose sighed and hoped neither would track the memory down. They had indeed met, albeit very briefly, at one of those dreadful parties at Lady Jane Hay-Hurt's. But he didn't think Agatha could put a name to this memory, for she had been busy talking to Lady Jane, who was in absolutely no danger of joining the Ardry-Plant line and raiding the inheritance. Lady Jane was literally long in the tooth, resembling as she did an Alsatian, and Agatha liked to push Melrose in her path, realizing that the Ardry-Plant fortune was perfectly safe. But in Lucinda, Agatha would see a possible adversary relationship; here was an eligible woman who had crossed Agatha's field of vision and had the temerity not to withdraw from the field. She was youngish and nice and merely plain. Melrose hoped that nothing would jog his aunt's memory because then she would recall having met Lucinda's mother, Sybil, with whom his aunt had had a wonderful time sitting on Lady Jane's settee, demolishing teacakes and characters.

"No, you haven't," said Melrose, putting a dead stop to speculation. "Miss St. Clair somewhat resembles Amelia Sheerswater." It was a name plucked from air. But it would make Agatha wonder about this *new* addition to the ranks of Melrose's women. "We're just having a drink; what would you like?"

Lucinda St. Clair drew her brown hair away from her face and appeared to be in deep colloquy with herself over the drink selection.

"How about sherry?" offered Vivian helpfully. "The Tio Pepe's very good."

As if Tio Pepe were a drink so rare, refined, and quixotic that it changed from bottle to bottle and pub to pub, thought Melrose. But might as well let Vivian do her thing. Lucinda nodded and Trueblood called to Dick Scroggs for the sherry before he settled back to plug a blue Sobranie into his holder.

Everyone smiled at Lucinda except Agatha, who still was scanning the St. Clair face for telling signs of the Sheerswater one.

It occurred to Melrose when Dick brought her Tio Pepe and stood there looking at the newcomer with his bar towel draped over his shoulder that perhaps the girl was uncomfortable amidst all of this attention. Indeed Lucinda looked from her glass to him and smiled weakly as if she thought she were expected to perform at this little pre-Christmas gathering, to jump up and recite something or tell a clever anecdote. What she did not realize was that they had all been saying pretty much the same thing to one another for years now and it was refreshing to see an unfamiliar face joining their ranks.

Melrose saw Lucinda sliding down a bit in her chair and decided to extricate her before the group all burst into carol-singing or something. He picked up his drink and hers, smiled, and excused both himself and her. "I really think Miss St. Clair has come to Long Piddleton for a bit of a talk with me."

When they were seated at a table near the fireplace, she began with another apology for presuming upon their brief acquaintance, and told him she was just on her way back from Northampton where she'd gone to pick up some materials and things. "For Mother. She's doing up a house in Kensington. You remember Mother?"

Didn't he just. Sybil had once been plain wife and mother before she'd taken up the artsy ways of the world of interior design. Typical of her, too, that she'd send the daughter to do the dog's work, running about with swatches of material, matching and measuring. As he remembered her, she seemed to prefer frocks without waists, all folds that hung aimlessly here and there. There was all the shine and glint in her complexion that Clinique could give her.

Melrose had met her again on one of his infrequent trips to London. He had befriended Lucinda, feeling something of the agony of a young woman with no social graces and the thin-legged, long-nosed look of a crane. She wore white and shouldn't have, as it only increased the image. Poor Lucinda managed to turn a deer park into a rain forest with her large, damp brown eyes. They had been staying at the hotel he liked. Tea at Brown's had escalated into dinner, where he told them about his visit at that very hotel with an American tour group. The story of those murders had enthralled them.

"What I remembered was that you seemed to have some experience with police—"

"Well, I do know one or two, yes. But I'm not really a dab hand at the business. Why?"

She took a long breath. "There's a friend of mine, see, who seems to have got himself in trouble. I just thought perhaps that you might be able to sort things out—Oh, I don't know. It's dreadful."

"What's happened? Who's the friend?" He was a little sorry he'd asked when she colored and looked away. The "friend" was undoubtedly more than a friend, or she hoped so.

"No one special, really," she said looking everywhere but at him. "A friend of the family. We've known him for ages. . . ." The whispery voice trailed off. "Did you read about that woman murdered in Mayfair? It was in the paper today."

The one Scroggs had talked about so juicily. "You don't mean your friend is mixed up in that? That *is* dreadful."

All in a rush and with a great deal of intensity she said, "I'm afraid that he might just be arrested or something. He was the last one to see the girl alive. Or at least that's what they're saying." From her large bag she drew out a copy of the same paper Scroggs had read them.

"Scotland Yard CID," he said after reading the account. "Is this your friend? The one who's 'helping police with their inquiries,' as they say?"

Lucinda St. Clair nodded. "I just thought that since you're so clever about these things—"

"If that's the impression I gave, I didn't mean to." He carefully folded the paper. He certainly had been decidedly unclever when he had helped Richard Jury on that last case. The memory still sent chills down his spine. "There's really nothing I can do. Civilians can't go messing about in police business, Lucinda." How many times had he been told *that* by Jury's superior?

It was a crestfallen look he got. "There's really no one else I can think of."

"Surely he has a solicitor—"

She nodded and looked desolate.

"I take it this gentleman is a very good friend."

The look of desolation only increased. "Yes."

Melrose thought for a moment. It wouldn't hurt, he supposed, to call Jury. "You've got to understand, though, that I can't do anything by way of interfering—"

"Oh, no one's thinking of your *interfering*. I just thought you might be able somehow to look at it from another perspective." She lost that rain-forest look for a moment. "Then you *will* come?"

"You mean to Sussex?"

"Somers Abbas. We could drive down together; I have my car—"

Melrose held up his hand. "No; I'll really have to think about this."

Lucinda sat back, looking more desolate than she had when she came in. "Will you call, then?"

"Of course." Melrose looked over to the table where Vivian, Trueblood, and his aunt still sat, the two women pretending not to be interested in the goings-on before the fireplace. Agatha was making a far poorer job of the pretense than was Vivian. Melrose smiled at the familiar trio in the bay window. Vivian smiled back and even wiggled her fingers in a friendly little wave. Perhaps her difficulty in crossing the Channel lay in some deep-rooted need to keep the little party intact. Benevolently she beamed at Lucinda.

He studied the girl. He felt a tacit agreement with Vivian that Lucinda St. Clair would probably never break up a party.

꧁꧂

On this rare December morning Melrose sat at the rosewood dining table, the *Times* folded beside his plate of eggs. He penned in two down and one across. But he was only giving part of his mind to the crossword; the rest was on the call he had made to Richard Jury, who had told him certainly, absolutely to go to Somers Abbas. That he was acquainted with someone who knew the Winslow family could be extremely helpful. And for all of the past help, well, Jury thought he deserved a knighthood. A bit redundant, perhaps, but anyway . . .

"I doubt very much that Chief Superintendent Racer would oblige with a knighthood. I doubt very much that Racer has been pleased. . . ."

Melrose looked down the length of the table and out the French windows that on this unseasonable day had been opened. Their creamy curtains billowed slightly in the breeze. Beyond the window he caught a glimpse of the serpentine path that wound through the grounds and down which he loved to stroll. All of those grounds out there—the wide expanse of gardens, the silver wintercrust of the lake, the yew hedges and willows —reminded him of the walk he had taken with Lucinda St. Clair at Lady Jane's party. Melrose could imagine, all the while, Sybil St. Clair watching with the patience of a puma straddled on a branch, waiting for the least flicker of movement from the quarry below. It was maddening to feel sorry for Lucinda, and impossible not to. She had, of course, been delighted that he was coming. And in face of all her mother's objections, Melrose had insisted at a room at the local inn.

He sighed and looked up, his eye moving round the walls and the portraits there that hung in such stately procession that the whole crowd of them might have been on its way to Westminster Abbey. Viscount

Nitherwold, Ross and Cromarty, Marquess of Ayreshire and Blythedale, Earl of Caverness . . . one could hardly name them without pausing for a stiff drink in between. His eye came to rest on the portrait of his mother, one of the most beautiful women he had ever seen, and one on whom that coronet must have weighed awfully heavily at the end. Filtered sunlight fell in dancing sequins on her pale gold hair, and humor was written all over her face.

He smiled. His mother, if not the Queen, he was sure had been pleased. . . .

"More coffee, m'lord?" asked Ruthven, Plant's paradigm of a gentlemen's gentleman, who had been in the family practically as long as the portraits on the walls. He held the silver pot aloft.

Melrose shook his head and put down his pen. "No thanks, Ruthven. I'd better be on my way." He pocketed his gold-rimmed spectacles and shoved back his chair.

"Will you be requiring the Flying Spur or the Rolls, sir?"

Melrose looked again at the portrait of Lady Marjorie. Was she smiling? "You know, Ruthven, I think anyone who's asked a question like that should be shot."

7

⮑❧❧⮐

THE last time Jury saw him, Brian Macalvie put his foot through a
jukebox. Today, at least, he was only playing it. For a man whose
sentiments ran toward moving through his men like Birnam Wood
and shouting at suspects, the divisional commander showed a remarkable
affinity for old songs and soft voices. It was probably Macalvie's choice
now that filled the Running Footman with its whispery *tristesse.*

He barely raised his eyes from the menu of songs when he spoke. "Hi,
Jury. Took you long enough." Macalvie slotted another ten-p piece into
the jukebox and hit the side when it didn't respond.

Jury could have run all the way from headquarters like the footman in
the huge picture that gave the pub its name. However fast he was, it
couldn't be fast enough. Time did a peculiar dance around Macalvie; he
picked up exactly where he left off. Two years ago, ten minutes, it made no
difference. Just as last year's murder was still today's news for Macalvie.
He never gave up.

Jury smiled. "The world wags by three times, Macalvie: God's, yours,
and Greenwich Mean."

Macalvie might have been checking his watch against the other two
because he shook it before he nodded. "Yeah. Have a beer. Just be careful
of the Gopher; it'd take the scales off a brontosaurus." He picked his pint
from the top of the jukebox and walked to a table beneath the painting.

When Jury came back with his own pint, Macalvie was standing and
drinking and studying the painting. "That's what we are, Jury, messen-
gers. Good news, bad news—people'd complain no matter what we
brought." He sat down. "Where's Wiggins?"

For a divisional commander who was his own one-man police force
because he couldn't put up with the slightest show of foot-dragging or
malingering, it was surprising that he got on so well with Wiggins. As

good a man as Wiggins was, he could be sluggish. Sickness wouldn't slow Macalvie down any more than a flea on a cheetah.

Macalvie brought out a cigar. The cellophane crackled like Macalvie's eyes. A walking conflagration with its roots in his Scotch-Irish ancestry spiked by a strong predilection for American cop films.

"Why aren't you chief constable yet, Macalvie?"

"Beats me," he said, with no trace of irony. "I would've got here sooner, only that train from Dorchester stops for chickens."

"You got here fast enough, considering we found the girl early this morning. I take it you think there's a connection—"

"Of course. Sheila Broome, found on a stretch of road beyond Taunton. For ten months I've been waiting for the other shoe to drop."

"You were sure it would? And Ivy Childess is the shoe?"

Macalvie shot him a look. "Yes."

"I don't want to tread on your theory, Macalvie—"

As if you could, the look said.

"—but murderers aren't all serial killers, and women get mugged every day. I don't much believe in startling coincidences."

"Oh, *come* on. You don't believe this started out as a mugging any more than I do."

True, he didn't. "I'm just more conservative, Macalvie."

"No wonder you got to be superintendent, Jury."

Jury ignored that. "So tell me about this Sheila Broome."

"She set out on the night of twenty-nine February to go to Bristol. That's according to her mum, only she told Mum she'd got a ride. To Bristol, that is. Since none of her friends knew anything about her leaving town and no one gave her a ride from around here, we figured she was getting lifts from along the road. She was *not* prissy Priscilla. There was nothing unusual about her—she snorted coke and slept around, her friends said. Age, twenty-six, hardly a schoolkid, never married. Pretty in a sulky way; not very likeable; did two O levels and then quit, so not ambitious, either. Worked at a pub in the new part of Exeter and didn't tell the landlord she was quitting. She put me in mind of an old newspaper; you could have blown her to Bristol, and no one would notice."

"What is it about the murder that makes you think it was more than Sheila Broome being in the wrong place at the wrong time?"

"Because she wasn't robbed and she wasn't raped. And they were out of the car, both of them, smoking grass in the woods. Now, if you were tooling along looking over the hitcher situation, what'd you be looking for? Sex or money or both. But with Sheila it's neither. I think it was someone who knew her; could have been a man, could have been a woman. I think it was someone *looking* for her—"

"That's a chancy way to get your victim, waiting until she hitches a ride."

"If you're not in a hurry, it's a swell way. Removes both of you from home ground."

"But the scarf; that doesn't sound premeditated, Macalvie. He just used the available means."

Macalvie got up and collected their glasses. "Oh, I imagine he had something else, a stocking, a gun." He went off to fill the glasses and, while he was waiting, to play the jukebox.

The Running Footman wasn't crowded; a few couples, a half-dozen singles that looked pleasant and not hurting for money. Jury supposed you weren't if you lived in Mayfair.

Macalvie walked back to the table, where they sat for a moment drinking and listening to the honey-voice of Elvis Presley. Elvis was Macalvie's favorite.

"Like I said, she wasn't robbed. She was carrying about seventy quid in a rucksack, another ten or eleven in her jacket. There was a gold watch, strap broken, in the pack and a couple of rings on her fingers."

"What about cars, drivers? Did you find anyone?"

"There was a lorry driver. I wouldn't have found him except for a waitress in a Little Chef who thought she remembered Sheila Broome's face, not so much because of the face itself, but because she was wearing a vest the waitress fancied and asked her where she got it. Electric blue, it was. And she remembered the artic because it was so big it took up nearly half the car park. Lucky for the driver that the waitress watched when they left; she said he must have started off with Sheila, but when Mary-the-waitress looked out the window, Sheila was stepping down from the cab. She could hardly see through the fog; it was that neon-blue vest. Then Sheila was trying to hitch another ride in front of the petrol station next to the cafe."

"And she didn't see anything else? No car stopping?"

Macalvie shook his head. "Next time she looked, she didn't see Sheila. Now, tell me about Ivy."

Jury told Macalvie the little they knew. Nodding his head in the direction of the side street, he said, "You've had a look, I suppose."

"Of course."

"It was two or three hours later that she was found."

"'Hours'? You ought to be on my forensics team."

"Thanks."

"No problem. Patience on a monument, Jury, that's me. Go on." Before his patience could be pressed into service, Macalvie turned to the table beside them and told the occupants to hold it down. They just stared.

"Princess and the pea is more like it. How many mattresses do you sleep on, Macalvie? The last her boyfriend saw of her she was standing in that doorway over there"—Jury nodded toward the entrance—"doing a slow burn." Jury told him about the interview with David Marr.

"Cab-driver said she flagged him down and then changed her mind?" Jury nodded.

"Cab-drivers can't see. All you have to do is grab a taxi to know that."

"Let's assume this one could," said Jury dryly. "It's not much of an alibi, anyway."

"How true. So this makes two."

"But muggings happen every day, a murder here and a murder in Devon—"

"Come on. We've just been *over* that. No rape, no robbery."

"Those are *un*knowns, Macalvie. The only *known* here is the way they were garroted."

"What more do you want? A bootprint on her forehead? It's like I said."

Like he said, thought Jury. Case open. Theory closed.

PART II

Reverie

8

❧

SHE spent the morning and part of the afternoon in the shops, not
buying, only looking, and after a while not seeing much of what she
looked at. In an antiques shop in the Lanes, she picked up a miniature, one of several on a black walnut table, and opened the heart-painted
top to read the legend inside: *Love Always*. Kate disliked these little, porcelain boxes that had no purpose but to sit on dressing tables or in escritoires
gathering dust. Her mother had collected them, tops painted with ribbons,
flowers, hearts, in that rather vague if feverish excitement her mother
affected in nearly everything she did.

So Kate was surprised to find herself in another part of the shop looking
at the old books, still holding the miniature in her hand. She must have
been carrying it long enough to draw the riveted gaze of the shopkeeper to
her. He had appeared again in the opening above the half-door to the room
beyond, his hands clasped behind him, staring at her like a guard from a
castle keep. Kate imagined that he thought she meant to nick it and she
was embarrassed enough that she turned it over to see the price. Twenty
pounds. It was not even a good example of its kind: the heart was threaded
with scratches, the gilt round the oval top was flaked. Indeed, it might not
even have been an original, but under the censorious stare of the owner,
she felt compelled to tell him she'd have it. Of course his manner altered
accordingly, the gaze shifted, the tone when he spoke was as cottony as the
small square placed into an overlarge box to act as a cushion.

It was easy enough to explain to herself when she was outside on the
pavement once more. Another little gift to appease the gods. What a conscience she must have, she thought, standing there outside the shop with
its partly shuttered windows. If she had ever tried to do anything criminal,
it would have caught her out immediately. How had her parents, both
shallow, feckless dilettantes, managed between them to fashion it? Far

more artistry had gone into this paste momento she held. She smiled grimly, pulled up the high collar of her lamb's wool coat, and started down the narrow street toward the ocean. Her conscience put her in mind of some medieval chalice of the sort she remembered seeing at the Victoria and Albert. An elaborate, supposedly splendid (but Kate thought vulgar) liturgical icon, heavily chased with gold beading, studded about with jewels. Her conscience, she thought ruefully, was as impractical and flashy as her sister, Dolly.

Kate maneuvered the narrow space between a Ford Granada with its bonnet up and the drab window of a boutique. The snow had had time to turn to slush, and the shoppers sluggish. None of the faces that she passed looked pleased with their errands or with their glittery surroundings. It was old glitter anyway, not new. The Royal Pavilion was banked in by scaffolding, and a wide, blue hoarding covered part of its front while it underwent repair. How many hundreds of pounds must be going into keeping these impractical, flashy minarets and turrets up. Kate thought again of Dolly.

No one except herself had forced Kate into those years of nursing their father, so she shouldn't blame Dolly for getting off scot-free. A flat in London, a score of lovers, and enviable looks were the rewards of self-indulgence—not to mention the money itself. Kate did not feel any bitterness with regard to her sister; Dolly had done nothing by way of manipulating the old man into leaving her the lion's share of the inheritance. It had long been clear that he would favor the child who, short of being the son, most resembled himself.

Kate had watched the progress of her father's illness over the years uncoil and make its slow way through tissue and bone. Still to the end the society of others had been his vocation; he drank champagne at breakfast and Glenfiddich at tea. Illness and dissipation had turned him into a hollow-cheeked, wasted man who looked twenty years older than he was, one whose mind had clouded over at the end: he had "visions," he said. The visions were usually uncomplimentary to his elder daughter, thought Kate wryly, and undoubtedly helped along by the Glenfiddich.

What had surprised Kate and what now all but overwhelmed her was the knowledge that it hadn't made any difference and that if her years of servitude had been intended as some sort of sacrificial offering, she had to face now the fact that there had been no gods to appease. Brighton beach in the winter dusk and the hard, dark shell of the sea was not the place to mitigate against her terrible disappointment at the lack of freedom she felt. That was something she had been sure she could have counted on, a sense of freedom and release. Now she was able to go anywhere and to live as she liked. She had made all sorts of plans before her father's death that she meant to put into motion when he was dead. Now she watched them idle there at the ocean's edge as if trying to grab hold or gain purchase on the shingle, breaking and pulling back, and breaking again. The romantic fancies became as repetitive as the collapsing waves and as dull and cold, too. A heavy drapery of fog covered the Palace Pier, hiding the flaking white paint, the rust. It had grown dimmer and dustier with the years, like the Pavilion back there. The West Pier farther away had been closed to visitors; it was dangerously in need of repairs. Away in the distance, floating like a shadow on the water, it looked delicate and fragile, made of matchsticks.

Kate went down the stair to the long seawalk, past the Arches beneath the King's Road, where most of the amusements were closed up now. She nodded to a young man who was painting the facade of the Penny Palace, painting bright marine blue pillars on its front. It was one of Kate's favorites, with its old machines that evoked so much of a Victorian Brighton. When her sister was small, she had loved to walk along the seafront with their father, past the Arches, licking ice cream or a stick of Brighton rock. But why her sister, who came down from London rarely, had appeared in Brighton now, Kate couldn't understand. On an impulse, Dolly had said.

Kate walked on to the next set of steps leading up, the carryall holding some chops and the wrapped-up box, hitched on her wrist and her hands stuffed deep in her coat pockets. She could feel a frayed seam. Whenever Dolly came down from London Kate grew more sensitive to things like her seven-year-old coat or an outmoded frock. Dolly stopped short of actual wardrobe trunks, but the several cases she would bring for her short stays bulged with outfits that spent their time in the cupboard, since there was nowhere they could go festive enough for turquoise silk or a fox-fur collar. Kate wondered sometimes if Dolly were still caught back in days of dress-up and blind-man's-buff.

Why had Dolly come? A man, perhaps. Dolly had never had good luck with men, beautiful as she was. Well, that might have been part of it. Too beautiful. Perhaps because of the difference in their ages the two had never been close, and Kate supposed she had resented the baby sister and little girl that Dolly had been. She must have, but Kate couldn't really remember, though she would have been twelve when Dolly was born. A very awkward twelve that had replaced an ungainly eight and in turn a square-jawed, dubious-seeming child of five. In the photographs Kate saw herself always as hesitant, standing on the edge of the occasions that prompted the photographs, as if she'd strayed into the family circle grouped against the dark backdrop, Dolly centered there and always dressed in something soft with tucks of organdy or spills of ribbon.

Dolly spent her visits trailing what could have been a trousseauful of negligees and velvet wrappers through the dark, high-ceilinged rooms of the house in Madeira Drive, sometimes sitting long enough to leaf through a magazine and always with a cigarette and a cup of tea. Dolly was so much like their mother that Kate had once or twice felt a surge of panic, seeing her in the shadowed hall or in the dark of the stairwell. It was no wonder that their father had doted on her, had exaggerated notions about Dolly's career, and fantasized about her life in rough approximation to those fantasies he had had about his own. They were fantasies that Dolly fed, not for any gain other than that she fed her own ego in the telling.

For professional reasons, she said, she had changed the spelling of their name to "Sands." It was easier to remember, looked simpler when the name flickered on the television screen at the end of the news report. Dolly had done well, very well. She had popularized something pretty dull.

Kate switched the carryall to her other hand, finding it a tiresome burden. The rashers and chops were best quality and probably half again as much as the price she would collect for the room. Dolly had been extremely put out to find that the house, old and dark but still elegant, was being turned by Kate into a bed-and-breakfast. They didn't need the money, she had complained, and taking in roomers seemed terribly lower class.

Privacy. Kate had always heard her sister complain before of too much privacy—not even a servant to bring Dolly her early morning tea. Since Dolly never rose in the morning before nine, Kate didn't know to what use the morning would have been put.

Kate made for the promenade and the news agent she patronized, where she bought a *Times* and a piece of Brighton rock. It was a sweet she had loved as a child before they had moved here permanently, when they had come (as her father liked to say) for the season—as though those were the Edwardian days of parasols and tea at the Royal Pavilion.

She walked toward Madeira Drive. Round and round in her mouth she turned the rock candy, its cloying sweetness like the aftertaste of childhood.

Dolly sat at the kitchen table, smoking and drinking tea and occasionally reading a tidbit from a review of a new American film as Kate cut up some potatoes and swede. They might have presented a picture of conviviality, even intimacy, to a stranger. Kate knew they were neither. She had said almost as much, asking Dolly why she bothered with this Brighton trip now their father was dead. The answer had been a stock one, that she didn't want Kate to be "on her own" for the holidays. It was all dead dialogue out of one of Dolly's own television programs.

Leaning her chin on her cupped hand, Dolly said, "I don't know how you stand it, Kate. You should sell up and come to London and get a flat."

"And do what?" Uninformed advice always irritated Kate. Dolly's was always that sort, suggesting that changing her life was of no more moment than handing over a claim ticket at the lost luggage counter.

"Oh, you'd find something," Dolly said vaguely, her eye returning to the social page. "You've got the education and you're really good-looking when you fix yourself up."

Kate turned up the flame on the cooker and positioned the pot with the basin over it. She laughed briefly. "Thanks for *that*. But when anyone says, 'Fix yourself up a bit,' that generally means a thorough turnout, like spring cleaning. The face will of course have to go. And the results of my A-levels dusted off and displayed—" She was getting angry. It was what she felt to be Dolly's total indifference to her masked by this spurious interest that made her situation stand out in sharp relief. "You haven't really thought about it. There's something a little mean about dragging out my dubious qualifications for this hypothetical something." Loneliness washed over her in waves. She felt she was back looking out over the sea again, not here in a warm kitchen.

Dolly's silence in face of this little outburst made Kate turn to look at her. She was looking out of the window with much the same intensity of Kate looking out over the sea.

"Dolly?"

Her sister turned. In the clear skin Kate saw little lines etched, worrisome little lines.

"Is something wrong?"

"No, nothing." Dolly shook herself and went back to reading her paper. Then she said, "I don't like the idea of turning this into a bed-and-breakfast. It's so—"

"Lower class?" Kate felt the anger dissipate. She turned back to the cooker. "It gives me something to do."

"And what do you know about the people you take in?"

"Not much. But I don't take many, you know."

Her sister arranged the lime-green nightdress in folds over her good legs, and the shift in posture accentuated the play of light across her breasts. It was all unconscious, Kate knew. The way she now held a match straight up to the tip of a fresh cigarette, the way she lowered her lashes, smoothed her hand over her pale gold hair. Then she rose and stretched, saying she thought she'd go up and have a bath and wash her hair.

As the slippers tapped down the hall, Kate sat down with her coffee and pulled the newspaper around, looking it over. Another drop in the economy, a shocking rise in rape cases, a child abused, a minister disrupting a cabinet meeting, a murder in Mayfair. Nothing ever changed much.

9

THE sign of the Mortal Man made the dusk hideous with its creak and clangor, swinging precariously above the road that wound about the village green. The gentleman pictured on the trembling sign was appropriately depicted, his gouged eyes seeming to reflect not so much on his own mortality as that of the sign. It was an old gallows sign, the sort that was made illegal over a century ago because of the traffic hazard. Probably no traffic hazarded the narrow lane crossed by the beam on which it swung.

From the outside, the Mortal Man wore much of the look of the country inn—black-and-white Tudor timbering and thatched roof. Inside, one of these beams was in the process of being hammered to splinters by a spindly young man up on a ladder. As Melrose looked left to the lounge and right to the saloon bar, he thought the inn had been caught in the middle of being taken apart or put back together again. Wood paneling leaned against the bar, a gold-framed mirror sprightly with cupids was in sore need of resilvering, a stained-glass window looked recently boarded up.

The hall was appropriately dark, with its thread of turkey carpet running along to a gloomy staircase. A porcelain leopard appeared to be guarding the dining room to his left. To his right a half-moon-shaped desk was attended by a burly man who was arguing with an unseen opponent, and through the archway to Melrose's left, the inn's personnel came and went—a maid with saucy curls demanding her wages of the gentleman behind the counter, who turned her back with vituperative rhetoric; a woman with a saucepan; a boy with a notebook followed by a muddy, hybrid hound; a thin girl with a mop and a slack look both in face and dress.

The dog welcomed the new guest by grabbing his trouser cuff and hanging on for dear life until the owner rousted him with a kick. Nathan

Warboys (for so he had introduced himself) then stood with his arms splayed over the counter under a sign reading *Reception,* with the intention of giving Melrose a hearty one by letting him in on the family secrets.

"And my Sally. It's a treat, it really is, and 'er comin' in night after night lookin' like the leavin's of a dogfight. Thought that'un 'ud stay on the shelf, I did, but no, she's got t'be gettin' up t'mischief just like the other. 'Ang about, 'ang about, now. Got to sign this, it's the law, mate." Whereupon he thwacked a card down for Melrose to fill in, and hit the bell with such force it sprang from the counter. This was by way of summoning the young lad with the terrier panting with the expectation of another go at the ankle. During their trudge up the narrow staircase, whose creaks and crepitations echoed the sign outside, the boy introduced himself as William Warboys. The dog's name was Osmond. Midway in this tortured ascent of a staircase only fit for one, Osmond had hitched his steel jaw to the toe of Melrose's shoe and no manner of shaking could dislodge him; to lift the shoe was to lift Osmond, who hung as tenaciously as a high-wire artist without a net. When William swung the bag at the dog, it slid from his hands and slapped Melrose on the shin on its dive down the dark tunnel of stairs.

Looking out from under the dripping thatch of the Mortal Man, Melrose was still rubbing his shin, and wondering if the tibia was in one piece. There was an unfamiliar rasping sound coming from his knee joint, an echo of the gallows sign.

He saw that the dull rain hadn't stopped, nor the fog lifted. The pavements were unpeopled, the green across the way uninhabited except for some geese and swans gliding on the pond, their white feathers threading in and out of the fog like graveclothes. The Norman church at the green's center looked buckled up and riveted shut. He made out the dimly lit windows of a cafe and a cluster of cottages with the same thatched roofs of the inn, all so close they looked stitched together.

Lucinda St. Clair had told him he would be collected for drinks at seven. He was glad it was drinks and not tea, for he was drinking that right now. He had not ordered it, but it had been brought nonetheless by the shapeless Sally Warboys, crockery dancing on the tray in her uncertain hands, tea slopping out from the pot and wetting the napkin. Even after she had set it down, tea dripped and china jangled, as if moved by a tremor of fear that Sally would take it up again. Melrose felt that the Warboyses, unable to direct their energy or even contain it, had unleashed it into the air, where it had then been absorbed by chairs, tables, glass, and cutlery. And now all of them were emitting it in nervous little jibs and jerks. Probably, he thought, it would all lead up to some Poe-esque denouement, where the Mortal Man, like the house of Usher, would be rent and fall apart, shuddering into dust. Every whack of the hammer on the floor below, every bellow of a Warboysian voice, told him this fancy must be so.

Hard on the heels of Sally came Mrs. Warboys, a stubby woman who moved like an eggbeater in fits and starts of stirring the log in the little fireplace, sending a burning particle onto the threadbare rug, which flamed up. They managed between them to stomp out the fire, but in the excitement Mrs. Warboys dropped the poker on Melrose's arch. She apologized and went about whipping a dresser set into place, sending the two glasses there crashing to the floor. Assuring him that Bobby would clean that up, she jerked together the muslin curtains and tore out one end of the rod so that the whole thing drooped pitifully. Her work done, she would now send up Bobby to undo it.

Up came Bobby with the hammer in his hand and a determined look on his face. He would certainly beat that curtain rod back into place, he said, until Melrose convinced him that he had a migraine headache and didn't care who looked in the window, anyway. Thwarted in his dedication to his hammer, Bobby shot Melrose a dark look and left.

Bobby's place was taken by William, who came with notebook and pencil like a plumber to give an estimate on fixing the toilet. From the bathroom came a tearing sound and a thump: William had slipped in the water from the overflowing toilet and fallen in the bathtub, taking the shower curtain with him in an attempt to keep his balance.

Melrose was beginning to wonder if a stay at the Mortal Man was so short-lived that each member of the family had to see the guest at least once before he died.

When the door had slammed behind William, Melrose thought that must be all of them, until he heard the scratching at the bottom of the door.

His welfare, he saw, depended upon his getting out.

There was little to see in the dark beyond the saloon bar's window, but Melrose thought it a safe place to stand, for if he suddenly toppled perhaps some passerby would see him and go for help. Fog drifted in threads round the street lamp, and lay like a canopy over the pavement, giving an oddly truncated look to the person wading through it, a tall man in a muffler and deerstalker. His face was long and sad and the pouches under the eyes reminded Melrose of Osmond. He shook Melrose's hand and introduced himself unhappily as St. John St. Clair, Lucinda's father. Perhaps it was having to trip over that name that made St. John St. Clair look so sad and grave.

They walked across the road to the large old car and once in it, St. John St. Clair began as if no time were to be lost in filling in the gaps in Melrose's store of knowledge about pickles. He was, apparently, a pickle baron, and was quite trenchant in his observations of the hopelessness of such a suzerainty. Not a good year for gherkins, seemed to be the top and bottom of it. He said this while grinding the very stuffing out of the gearbox of his ancient Morris.

St. Clair slapped the gearshift with the heel of his hand and the car lurched forward and they darted away from the curb. A patch of ice spun them sideways and slapped Melrose against the dashboard. St. Clair nearly strangled the wheel getting the Morris back on course without missing a beat in his pickle-talk.

Melrose sighed and mumbled and rubbed his shoulder. As he wondered if he'd leave Somers Abbas alive, he tried to be sympathetic. To have three unmarried daughters (so St. Clair had gravely informed him) all living under one's roof and to have devoted one's time and talents to pickles were perhaps not cheering thoughts for a winter's night.

10

By the time the Morris slid to a stop in front of the Steeples, had Melrose had any stock in Shrewsbury Pickles and Fine Relishes he would have called his broker immediately, so grim were St. John St. Clair's prognostications for the fate of his company. Perhaps the dark months ahead (for so his host painted them) goaded him into several flirtations with danger on the roads: they had only just missed a collision with a wagon, an overhanging willow, and a stone wall; and now the car had shaken the snow from the privet hedge and nearly toppled an urnful of frozen stalks that sat at the edge of the broad steps.

Definitely a Warboysian ride, he thought, as he swept a bit of boxwood from his coat and a twig from his shoe and followed St. John St. Clair up wide iced-over steps inviting death.

Sybil St. Clair rose to greet him, hands outstretched and—given her dress—flags flying. The frock seemed to consist largely of loose ends and scarves that looked about to flutter off through the long drawing room. Melrose could see that it had been a very handsome room with rosewood paneling and an Adam ceiling. "Had been" because Sybil, who fancied herself a decorator, had refurbished it in the Art Deco style: there was entirely too much of blue glass and green marble. He remembered now that she had quite an extensive clientele eager for her services. He couldn't truly imagine anyone with any taste going to Sybil, who managed to put together rooms that reminded him of old cinemas. Indeed, she herself put him in mind of an old cinema star, with her frock of scarves and winged hairdo totally wrong for her plump face.

He could do nothing but take her two ringed hands in his own and accept their affectionate little squeeze as if he were an old and very dear friend. With her whispery sort of speech, Sybil St. Clair had a way of fashioning intimacy out of the briefest acquaintance.

Fortunately the St. Clair daughters did not share their mother's tendency to rush and gush, Lucinda being too well bred and shy, and the others too haughty and holy in turn. The middle girl was named Divinity, and she sat pale and righteous by the fireplace on a hard chair; the youngest was Pearl, who kept herself on display on a giltwood fauteuil. Melrose wondered if the mother had meant to put a price on one head and a wimpel on the other. Pearl fingered a very long and very costly strand of them, and Divinity offered a limp hand and a lopsided smile probably meant to suggest that this little gathering was beneath her heavenly office.

It was unfortunate that Lucinda, a good-natured and honest girl, had got her father's long face and mournful eyes. And her dress was hardly flattering to her, though it might have been to her father's business; it was an ugly shade of gherkin green that, in the firelight, reflected up and deepened her sallow complexion.

Said Sybil to Melrose, "We did so want our neighbors, the Winslows, to come. But they couldn't make it. We try to do what we can to help." Sybil sighed and took an intricately decorated canapé from an Art Nouveau tray.

Before Melrose could ask why their neighbor was in need of help, St. John St. Clair said, "It would be nice if she were nearer." He passed a critical eye over the canapés and selected two, which he put on his small plate. "—or if someone were nearer. I don't know why we need all of this land." He sighed.

"Good heavens, Sinjin, *you're* the one who wanted to buy here. *You're* the one who wanted land, you said."

"*Good* land, yes," said St. Clair.

"What do you mean? It's perfectly good land." Sybil offered Melrose a grating little laugh as if assuring him their land was as good as anybody's.

"We can't grow anything properly. Peters is always telling me that nothing will grow in this soil."

"Don't be ridiculous. We've a perfectly *beautiful* garden. Marion was remarking on it just the other day—"

"It is the Winslow garden that is perfectly beautiful, my dear. Not ours. And of course poor Marion would say that, she is the soul of kindness. Her floribunda would win ribbons. All we can grow is creepers because they seem to withstand mildew and black spot very well, of which we have an ample supply." He said this with a sort of resignation that bespoke long acquaintance with the vicissitudes of blight and black spot. Then he bit into his cucumber sandwich, frowned at it, and with a sad headshake returned it to his plate.

"Oh, Lord! Both of you," said Pearl, adjusting a little pillow behind her back. "I doubt Mr. Plant wants to hear about our garden and land!"

Which sounded more sensible than he expected Pearl to be until she added, "I'm sure Mr. Plant has gardens of his own."

"I'm sure he has, too, and better," said St. John, rather sadly. "Can't I freshen your drink, Mr. Plant—?"

"Thank you."

"—although I doubt very much you care for more gin. It's really not up to standard. The whiskey might be better. A little." He raised the whiskey decanter.

"The gin seems fine, thanks."

St. Clair raised a curious eyebrow. "Really? Well . . ." With some doubt he went about refilling the glasses as he continued talking about gardens here and there. "Of course your gardens in Northants would be considerably finer than ours—"

Melrose laughed. "Now there you are absolutely wrong, Mr. St. Clair. Sussex is the place for gardens. Always has been."

Handing Melrose his glass and reseating himself he said, "Oh, yes indeed. Certain parts of Sussex. But here in Somers Abbas the wet just drowns everything in its path." He tasted his fresh drink and frowned.

"That's ridiculous, Sinjin. And let's stop all this talk about *gardens*—"

"Heavens, yes," said Divinity, as if the word had come down from there.

"We did want the Winslows to come this evening—" In the midst of studying over the label on the bottle of malt whiskey, St. John said, "I can understand why poor Marion would not want to socialize—"

"Poor Marion?" said Lucinda. "I should think it would be poor *David.*"

Sybil leaned forward and said to Melrose eagerly, "You heard what happened?"

"Really, Mother," said Divinity. "We shouldn't be talking common gossip."

Replacing the bottle with a frown, St. John said, "I've nothing against gossip, nor rumor, just so long as there's no truth in it and, therefore, cannot damage a reputation through repetition." He sighed. "But in this case, one does wonder. David Marr has always been unlucky—well, but haven't they all? The unluckiest family I believe I know, even more so than my own. Edward had a bad marriage, didn't he, my dear? Wasn't her name Rose? And didn't she leave him flat? Yes, I believe she did. And there was the little girl, poor little Phoebe, who was killed in that accident. And we mustn't forget Hugh. Hugh is Marion's husband, but we seldom see him. Hugh keeps to himself in that house in Knightsbridge and does not come down." St. John sat there, sinking deeper into gloom and finally stopping, like a man in a cave striking match after match, only to watch each one, and finally the last one, gutter out.

"Hugh does not keep *precisely* to himself," said Sybil. "I don't think Marion will *have* him down—"

"Oh, but we shouldn't go talking about that, my dear. We do not absolutely *know* that Hugh has other women. Not more than one, surely. And now here's poor David, with his fiancée murdered."

"He wasn't *engaged* to her, Daddy," said Lucinda.

"How do you know that?" asked her mother.

"Marion told me. She met her the one time. At the London house. David and some others were there for drinks."

"You mean the girl was at the house?"

"Well, what's so odd about that?" asked Lucinda, incensed. "He was going round with her."

St. John was closely inspecting the plate of canapés. "It is too bad about those boys; they both should settle down. I don't care for this fish paste; it's not the brand we usually buy."

Pearl had left her seat to arrange herself before the fire, catching whatever she could of the leftover light spilling from Divinity's person. "Edward was supposed to have come this evening. He was to bring me his new book."

"But I've got it, my dear," said her father. "I believe it's in the car."

She pouted. Apparently, since Edward Winslow had not come with it, better it had not come at all. Now she would have no excuse for running to the Winslow house and collecting it herself. "Mr. Winslow is a writer?"

"A poet, yes," said St. John. "Unfortunately, poetry doesn't sell."

Sybil laughed. "It hardly needs to, with all of their money. Now, Mr. Plant, I'm sure you'll reconsider and stay with us."

This so caught Melrose by surprise he hadn't time to muster his forces before she continued.

"There's simply no reason why you should stay at the Mortal Man when we've a half-*dozen* perfectly lovely rooms."

"He wants to stay there, Mother," said Lucinda. She looked unhappily at Melrose as her mother continued, obviously deaf to any attempt to scotch her plan.

"Oh, Lucinda, don't be ridiculous. You think you're putting us out," she said to Melrose, "but you aren't at all and I can't imagine why Lucinda didn't insist you stay here—"

"Mother, he doesn't *want*—"

"Lucinda, please. I've had the maid fix up a room with a perfectly marvelous fireplace—"

"It smokes," said St. Clair, putting his whiskey aside.

Melrose was actually becoming alarmed when he saw Sybil St. Clair ring for their servant. "The inn is fine, Mrs. St. Clair, please don't—"

"It does *not* smoke, Sinjin. The fireplace was seen to by Parkins just this summer—"

"Parkins doesn't do a good job, my dear."

"Mother—"

"The Mortal Man is an architectural gem," said Melrose quickly, as the servant Peters came through the double doors. "And as I told Lucinda—"

"We can just have Peters get your things for you. He can take the car."

"I told Lucinda"—Melrose was practically strangling his whiskey glass —"I've a special interest in inns, and the Mortal Man is a remarkable example of the old coaching inn—"

"I shouldn't think so," said St. Clair, who was staring up at the ceiling. "I shouldn't think the Mortal Man was much of an example of anything."

"It's no trouble at all Mr. Plant. And it won't take more than a moment. Peters—"

Melrose's paean to the English inn rushed ahead (he hoped) of Peters's leaving for it. "You see I *always* stay at an inn whenever there's the chance. As a matter of fact, I'm doing a sort of study of the English inn. Why, only the church has a richer history—"

"Oh-ho!" said St. Clair, with a crimped little smile. "Not *our* St. Mary's I assure you—"

"—to sit before an open fire and see the copper catching the light; to drive through the coaching archway into the cobbled yard and imagine the strolling players of Elizabethan times—"

"Not the Mortal Man's, I shouldn't think. The milk-float lost a wing and got its sill torn off there; and as for strolling players, well . . . unless one thinks of the Warboyses in that way. They do tell me he sings. . . ."

Melrose hoped not. "The timbered frontage, the fittings, the cellars, the carved woodwork, the rafters and beams—"

"Dry rot and rising damp," said St. Clair, pleasantly.

Into this overlapping conversation came the ringing of a telephone from deep in the house, and Peters, duty calling him elsewhere, nodded and begged to answer the sound.

Melrose leaned back, as breathless as if he'd run the mile, and feeling between the Warboyses and the St. Clairs like an object to be sent here and there, bag and baggage, dropped and collected, dumped and thumped on, and generally traded for a mess of pottage.

11

~❧ ❧~

BREAKFAST was an occasion involving the usual hazards. He should have known that the juice would spill, the porridge tilt, and the mackerel slide and taken the precaution of wearing a bib.

As Melrose ate the mackerel he had rescued from his lap, he listened to the keening sound coming from the kitchen. It increased and diminished each time Sally Warboys slapped open the door to bring him another dish. It might have been the screech of a kettle forgotten on the hob or the youngest Warboys (there was a baby, too) with some intractable demand. There had already come from the kitchen the clatter of breaking crockery and the usual assortment of angry voices as the Warboyses took their battle stations.

Sally Warboys, in washboard gray, came out of the kitchen in her half-run, half-walk, to deposit Melrose's pot of tea, which struck the table edge and sent hot water splashing down the cloth, just missing his hand by an inch. To call the Warboyses accident-prone would have been to do them an injustice, he thought; there was something here that smacked of deeply rooted tribal behavior.

As he blotted a bit of grease from his cuff, he noticed that the lad who had done porter duty and dropped his bag had come into the dining room. This room was undergoing a Warboysian transformation, with Bobby up on his ladder swinging his hammer.

William sat at the table across the room. In another this might have been called a "respectful distance," but in a Warboys it looked like the first step in a campaign from which Melrose doubted he would emerge the victor. The boy sat stiff and staring, with a gaze so intent it pried Melrose's eyes up like a lever. He was assisted in this scrutiny by Osmond, who lay on the floor with his head on his paws, eyes unflinching. Melrose assumed this was tactical necessity on the dog's part, like a falling back of troops readying for a surprise attack. He wondered if there had ever been guests at the Mortal Man before he happened along, for none of them seemed to know what to make of one—whether to hold him hostage or kill him outright.

"Good morning," said Melrose cheerily. "It's William, isn't it?"

The boy responded swiftly and came over to the table. He sat down and placed a small notebook and pencil, or the stub of a pencil, beside the plate of buttered crumpet that Melrose had not ordered. When Melrose invited him to have one, he pulled the plate and marmalade pot over with an alacrity that would have made one think he'd been on prison rations up to now.

Melrose pointed toward his notebook. "Are you writing something?"

Mouth full of marmaladed crumpet, William nodded energetically. The Warboyses had trained themselves never to waste a gesture, apparently.

"What?"

"A story." He mounded some currant jelly on another crumpet. "I wrote one once and it won a prize."

"It did?"

"Ten pound. Mum bought a new frock."

"That's very generous of you, to give her your prize money."

"I didn't. She took it."

Since there was no rancor in the boy's tone, Melrose assumed that this was the usual Warboys transaction. "What's this story about?"

"Chillington's has this contest going and there's fifty pound prize money—"

Melrose frowned. "The only Chillington I know is a brewer."

William nodded. "They're the ones that have all of them pubs with squirrels in them—"

As William paused to put another dollop of jam on his crumpet, Melrose tried to imagine a pub filled with squirrels.

The boy continued. "You know, the Squirrel and Pickle, the Squirrel and Mouse . . . everyone has a squirrel. So they want a story about a squirrel they can put a little bit of on their beermats each month. Here—"

He reached in his pocket and brought out a square of cardboard, somewhat stained. There was a picture of a squirrel sitting snugly inside its tree cave, wrapped in a checkered bathrobe, reading.

"It's fifty pound prize money. Mum wants to put heat in the toilet. I hate it when I'm still sleepy and have to go down to the toilet. This morning there was ice on the chain."

"That *is* pretty rum."

"Can I have some tea?"

"What? Oh, yes. It still seems hot." Melrose took the precaution of pouring. "What have you got so far?" He nodded toward William's notebook.

William stopped slurping his tea and opened the notebook. " 'Sidney reared back. There was blood on his anorak. The strange shape disappeared into the bushes.' Sidney's the squirrel."

"An exciting story. Where did the blood come from?"

"I don't know."

"Is he dead? Or dying?"

"I don't know."

Melrose wondered if this was the way Polly Praed wrote her mysteries.

"Maybe his friend Weldon is dead," said William, licking marmalade from his knife.

"Who's Weldon?"

"A weasel."

It was beginning to sound like an X-rated version of *The Wind in the Willows.* "Did somebody kill Weldon?"

"I don't know. Probably. It could have been with a knife," he said, using his own for demonstration purposes.

Melrose moved his chair back. "Well, what's the body doing in the bushes?"

"I don't know."

Better that a Warboys work off the inherited tendency toward destruction even if his narrative did have a few holes in it. "I must say you've not much to be going on with. Anyway, you might be quite rich some day if you keep to your story-writing."

William said he cared nothing for riches; just that he would like some heat in the toilet.

"That seems reasonable. I wish you'd stop playing with that knife."

"I had a weasel once. It's out back. With the others."

" 'The others'?" Melrose was beginning to wonder if this was not an inn but a Hitchcock motel.

"That's right. In the graveyard. They die and I bury them." William dusted his hands of death and crumbs and rousted Osmond. "There's a lady and man wants to see you." He nodded backwards. "Out there in the hall."

"You mean they've been out there all of this *time?*"

"Told me to give you a message." William had got up, clearly bored and with an eye on the headier environs of the kitchen.

Melrose was on his feet. "What message?"

William studied his notes. "Don't remember. But you can just as well ask them." And he was off, followed by Osmond, who took a swipe at Melrose's ankle before his paws click-clicked off.

The man was Edward Winslow, and Melrose had come in on the tail end of a conversation he was having with Nathan Warboys, who left for the bangings and hammerings of the saloon bar.

They had come, said Lucinda, to collect Melrose for morning coffee. David was down from London.

Her expression when she spoke the name David reaffirmed Melrose's belief that love must surely be blind. He did not have to meet David Marr to wonder how any young woman could prefer another man to Edward Winslow.

He was extremely handsome—hair the color of tawny port, eyes like burning brandy. Perhaps it was their proximity to the bar and Nathan's fixation on his happy family of ales and liquors that put Melrose in mind of these spiritous metaphors. But the coloring was Winslow's, nonetheless. And the rest of him lived up to that richness. He was the type who'd be any man's mirror: you couldn't help looking at him without wanting to straighten your tie and curse your tailor. There was nothing fashionable about Winslow, and certainly nothing trendy. In his dark gold cashmere jacket and plain brown silk tie, he was the paradigm of unself-conscious elegance. He would wear a trench coat over evening clothes and think nothing of it.

And that the man could find conversational possibilities in a Warboys monologue was a mark of extraordinary inventiveness, even for a published poet.

As Edward Winslow smiled and shook his hand, Melrose could understand why Pearl nearly strangled on her necklace when Edward had failed to present his book personally.

Though thoughts of strangling were perhaps not in the best of taste, Melrose thought, as they walked out into the cold and the wet to Edward's car—a black BMW, of course, the Savile Row of cars. Not ostentatious, just well made and made to stick it. Melrose slid down in the back seat as the doors clunked shut, thinking of his Flying Spur, his Silver Ghost. Well, perhaps they could talk about poetry.

12

D AVID Marr was in the library getting himself drunk at ten o'clock. He was standing by a commode of lacquer and gilt bronze that looked as if it should have been in a museum instead of doing service as a drinks table.

Indeed, the entire Winslow library looked like a place in which Marshall Trueblood could have happily expired. If the house had seemed depressingly stark from the outside—rock-faced granite with all the weight of medievalism upon it overlooking a choked and tangled woods—this severity was not repeated here in the library. An Italian marble fireplace was flanked by panels of bas-relief; the upholstery was Italian cut-velvet; the wallpaper and draperies, William Morris; around the walls were family portraits, oils, watercolors, Belgian tapestries. Melrose would have liked to spend several hours with these bound volumes in arched recesses, and a few more hours studying the paintings and portraits. Beside a Belgian tapestry was what looked like a Pissaro, beside that a Millet. It was a warm and peaceful scene of a thatched-roofed inn, quite lovely, he thought, in spite of his present doubts that thatched-roofed inns could contribute to the general happiness of the world.

David Marr held up a bottle of vodka. "Care for a saltwater?" he said, as soon as they were introduced.

Melrose smiled. "Never heard of it."

"Two goes of vodka, same of ginger, splash of grenadine." He poured more than two measures of vodka into his glass. "It's romantic, makes me think of the sea. Of course"—he set down the bottle—"I leave out the grenadine. Actually, I leave out the ginger, too. Sure you won't join me? Ned? Lucinda?"

"No, thanks," said Edward Winslow. "I see you switched from brandy."

David Marr sank down on one of a pair of Queen Anne sofas, sliding down on his spine. He was a handsome man, and he looked like his nephew despite the difference in coloring. Edward was fair; he was dark, eyes glitter-black, chips of the night sky, intense. Too intense to make the drunken-playboy manner believable, the slouching position on the sofa anything but self-conscious.

As he measured out his drink with a frown of concentration, David said, "Lucinda says you're staying at the Mortal Man. And here you are, alive to tell about it." He put down the bottle, turned, and smiled at Melrose.

"Here I am, yes. Aren't people always swearing out complaints or suing them, or something? So far I've had three narrow escapes—my carpet very nearly caught fire, my suitcase fell on me, and my breakfast landed in my lap. The place is a minefield. But the Warboyses take it all in stride and soldier on."

"No one's sued them yet that we know of," said Lucinda. "But I don't think they get many overnight guests. How about that coffee, then?"

"Yes, I'd love some coffee. As for the guests: you might have seen them go in; but did you see them come out?"

David laughed, then asked Edward, "Where the devil are the servants?"

"Bunburying," said Ned Winslow, smiling.

"What, again?"

"What's bunburying?" asked Lucinda.

"Bunbury was Algie's mythical old friend; don't you remember? Anytime he wanted to leave London, he'd say old Bunbury was ill. Well, I shouldn't complain, I suppose I'm doing it myself. Anything to get out of London. I expect Lucinda's told you about what happened." He looked at Melrose, got up again, and headed for the vodka. "I'm glad to help police with their inquiries—" He smiled. "—but it's getting tiresome. If not actually dangerous."

"There's not a bit of evidence, David," said Lucinda. "They haven't found anything yet."

David stopped the brandy decanter in midair and said to her, "I like that 'yet.' It's not particularly reassuring to think tomorrow they'll find my fingerprints smeared all over Hays Mews."

"They won't," said Ned shortly, as he went to poke up the fireplace. He turned and rested his arm along the green marble, much in the manner in which he was posed in the portrait above. It was a portrait of the three of them—the woman there looked enough like David Marr to be his twin. Melrose could not put his finger on what was so compelling about the painting: it was perhaps what it said of the relationship between the three. Melrose wondered where the husband was. Perhaps St. Clair was right. "They won't because you had nothing to do with it," said Ned.

"If only the *police* would see it that way."

"They will."

David rolled his head, resting against the back of the sofa, back and forth, sighing. "Well, not to worry. It's just a damned nuisance being told not to leave the country. Why does one always want to leave the country when one is told not to? Why does one always have the urge to visit Monte Carlo or the Himalayas when someone insists one stay at home? Why—?"

"The Himalayas might do you good. The last time you were in Monte, Mother had to send money."

There was great good humor in Ned Winslow's tone. Melrose had the impression they all indulged one another's weaknesses.

David shrugged. "Maybe I shall do a Bunbury. Incidentally, Marion is having a lie-down; she's not feeling well. I hope it's not because of me. Where's the coffee, Lucinda?"

Lucinda went as she was bid, Edward to help her. Melrose wondered how she could think she had a chance with this man, who watched her departing back without a flicker of interest. It was too bad; Edward and Lucinda seemed a suitable couple, though he wondered why "suitability" had anything to do with it; love was not a well-cut suit of clothes.

"Lucinda says you're quite an authority on the French Romantics." He smiled. "About which I know sod-all. But did you know Edward is a poet." David rose with his glass; this time, however, he headed for the bookshelves rather than the commode. He drew out the volume Melrose recognized as Edward Winslow's. "You should read it."

"I have; Lucinda gave me the copy intended, I fear, for Pearl St. Clair."

David laughed. "I'm sure Pearl didn't mind; that relieves her temporarily of having to pretend she can read." He leafed through the book, and said, "It's so simple, Ned's poetry. I guess I mean old-fashioned or something. " *'Where have you gone to Elizabeth Vere—?'* " David snapped the book shut, replaced it, moved to the lacquer commode. "Ned isn't very happy. He should get married again."

"I'm a little surprised you'd think *that* an antidote for happiness." Melrose smiled. "In their refusal to gossip, the St. Clairs did manage to let slip that your nephew was once married . . . to a woman who was, well—"

"Not terribly reliable. No, Rose was not reliable at all." His smile this time was decidedly chilly, a crack in ice. "He's very deep, Ned. Not at all like me. I'm about this deep." He held up the bottle with the remaining measure of vodka.

"Oh, I'd say you're a great deal alike." Melrose looked up at the portrait above the marble mantel. "The artist who painted that seems to think so, too."

"Paul Swann. Well, he's known us for a long time, but I don't see that in the painting, really."

"He's a friend of yours?"

"Yes; he lives near me in Shepherd Market. Paul was in the Running Footman that night. Only he'd left, I think. If my memory of events weren't so clouded by this"—he held up the glass—"it would be easier. Fortunately, there's that telephone call to my sister."

Fortunately, thought Melrose.

After coffee, they stood in the entry hall, a vast expanse of walnut paneling and sweeping staircase. Ned Winslow was to return Melrose to the Mortal Man; Lucinda was to stay behind to keep David company. The only company that David seemed interested in was the fresh bottle of vodka he'd found.

It was down that staircase that the woman in the portrait came. She was tall and dark like her brother, her hair a shimmery mahogany, swept up on her head in a carelessly done knot, dressed in a velvet morning robe of deep sable brown.

If this was poor Marion, there was something to be said for the ennobling effects of misfortune.

Inclining her head toward Melrose, she apologized for not coming down earlier. "I have a fierce headache, Mr. Plant. I hope you'll pardon me." That she remained standing on the stairs testified to her intention of going up them again as quickly as possible. Still, she struck Melrose more as a withdrawn, distant woman than a cold one. And very well bred. After all, she hadn't needed to come down at all; she could merely have conveyed her regrets, or indeed said nothing. He thought she gave Lucinda a chilly look, probably for having gotten her son to invite this stranger here in the first place.

Melrose wished she would stay; he would have liked to get more of an impression of her, which was why she was leaving, probably. In the circumstances, he supposed she thought the briefer the acquaintance, the better.

"Good Lord, Marion," said David, "why do you give that layabout couple leave to go when you're not feeling well?"

She smiled, but the smile did little toward warming the high, cold brow. "Too tired to pour your own brandy, David?" There was no real recrimination in the tone. "Don't worry, they said they'd be back today or tomorrow."

"I don't think you should be here alone and fending for yourself, that's all."

"Well, now I have you to fend for me." The humor in her voice was mixed with concern.

The expression on David Marr's face was strange, looking up the staircase. A strained, almost rapt expression, as if he were looking but not hearing.

Indeed, Melrose thought, all of them in this moment of silence and studied attention might have been grouped here, sitting for the portrait in the library.

A telephone rang in the distance, and Edward made a move toward a door across the wide hallway.

"Oh, hell!" said David. "That's the police, I'd bet my last drink on it." As Edward disappeared through the door, David called, "Don't answer it, Ned, let the damned answering machine do it. That's what it's there—"

He must have realized what he'd said the moment the words were out, for he broke off abruptly and polished off the rest of his drink.

There goes the alibi, thought Melrose.

～✥～

"Is this the garden that Mr. St. Clair seems to feel is the happiest in Sussex?" asked Melrose. They had come to the end of a path that led through beeches to an informal garden at one side of which ran a long, serpentine wall overgrown with moss, covered in wisteria, and under the shelter of overhanging laburnum whose branches dripped rain.

Edward Winslow laughed. "Yes, this is it. It might be larger than his, but it's hardly impressive. Still, try to tell Sinjin that. If he owns it, it's dreadful. Modesty run amok. He's a nice man, though. Actually, I'm surprised that John manages to keep things in such good shape." Ned waved to the gardener, who seemed to be hacking away at a monkey-puzzle vine in the distance. "Crusty old beggar thinks he's Gertrude Jekyll; still, he docs a good job out herc. You scc the garden wall there?" Ned nodded toward the laburnum grove. "It's our family plot. Several great-aunts and my grandparents are buried there. And Phoebe."

"That must have been pretty dreadful."

Ned was silent for a moment, staring at the little graveyard. "We all loved Phoebe so much."

"I'm sure. I've never had children."

"Nor I. My wife didn't want any. Rose didn't much care for the country here. Actually, she didn't much care for me, I think, and the proximity to Mother. Mother can be, as you might guess, a formidable person. But she never interfered, never. It's just her presence. She can move us about, you know."

There was no resentment in his tone. Melrose could well imagine Marion Winslow "moving them about."

"One day I woke up," continued Ned, "and she was gone. I don't know where; she had talked about the States, about Canada. But she didn't bother leaving a note. So I don't know where, do I?"

"Where have you gone to . . . ?" Melrose could not help but think of the poem.

Ned looked from the graves to the wall to the sky. "There was another man, I'm sure. Didn't even know she'd been seeing him. Didn't even know *him.* That's how blind a poet can be."

"Or how blind a wife can be." Ned Winslow gave him the impression of a man who'd accepted the past as nothing but a missed train on a wasted journey; he would stand on the platform or travel through life with his cases empty.

Melrose had been carrying the small book of poems in his pocket and drew it out. He thumbed through the pages until he came to the poem David had mentioned.

"It's very old-fashioned, as David says. Rhyme, meter, quatrains."

"There is something to be said for what you call 'old-fashioned.' Here it is." Melrose read:

> *"Where have you gone to, Elizabeth Vere,*
> *Far from the garden, the blossom, the bole?*
> *Rain glazes the stream—"*

Melrose looked off toward a small stream partly shrouded in ice that meandered close to the garden wall. "It sounds like this place. Was it meant for someone in particular?" He returned the book to his pocket.

Ned stood looking off toward the grove of beeches, frowning. "A writer never really knows who he means, does he? Perhaps that really is blindness, not to know." He changed the subject. "If you knew David, you'd know it's impossible for him to have strangled that girl. Anyway, there's no reason, no motive. Ivy must've been killed by a mugger, someone like that. Wouldn't you think that the obvious answer?"

Ned Winslow looked at him as if Melrose were a magician who just might pull the right rabbit out of the hat. "If that were the case, the killer certainly didn't want much. There appears to be no motive."

"There's none with David, either. He had no motive."

Melrose thought of what Jury had told him of the women, Sheila Broome and Ivy Childess. " 'Then glided in Porphyria—' "

Ned reached out to pull a weed from between the stones of the wall. "That's an odd allusion. If you're thinking of David as a Porphyria's lover type—" Ned laughed. "Believe me, he hadn't any passionate attachment to Ivy Childess." He turned those molten umber eyes on Melrose. "And what about Porphyria herself?"

"Porphyria? She struck me as being rather pathetic."

"She struck me as being a bit of a tramp," said Ned, with a smile.

13

❝WHAT *is* the matter with you, Dolly? You've been in a sulk—
well, not that perhaps—on edge, more, ever since you
came here." And as Kate set the cup of tea and a toasted
tea cake before her sister, she wondered once again why Dolly *had* come.
Her visits up to now had been in the spring or summer, especially summer,
the clement weather and quieter ocean allowing her to show off her near-
perfect figure. "Job? Man? What?"

Dolly looked up at her sister. "Nothing's wrong. I'm just a bit under the
weather is all." She set about cutting up her tea cake.

"And speaking of being here . . . you know you're always welcome, of
course . . . but why now?"

Dolly sighed. "I should think that would be obvious. It's the Christmas
holiday, isn't it?"

Kate watched her lick the butter off her fingers, slowly, like a cat. Dolly
moved with a languor that was also catlike and totally at odds with her
temperament. The edginess of which Kate had just spoken was not unusual, except in its intensity.

"It's a man, isn't it?" With Dolly it usually was.

"No." She said nothing else as she pulled up the glove-leather high-
heeled boots. She fitted a magnificent white fur Cossack hat to her head
and shoved the ends of her hair up under it. She reminded Kate of a photo
of a Russian spring, cold light shining on ice and snow.

"Where're you going?" Kate was clearing away her tea things.

"Only to Pia's."

That was another thing, thought Kate. Dolly was forever waiting for
Fate to step in, always counting on the planets to tilt in her favor. Two
years ago it had been the medium, and following her fall from grace, the
astrologer and the reader of tarot. Pia, to whom Dolly was currently en-

trusting her future, was a clairvoyant with a reputation in Brighton for honesty. The astrologer had been safe. With all of the open doors in one's horoscope through which one's fate could exit, astrology generally *was* safe. Unfortunately, Pia Negra wasn't. She told her clients what she knew, good or bad. And in Dolly's case, Kate supposed it must be rather bad, for she often came back more nervous and anxious than when she'd left.

It must be a man, thought Kate once again. The wrong man, of course. Why was it Dolly, who could have probably any man she fancied, always chose the wrong one? Married, sometimes; too old, sometimes; sometimes both. Whenever she told Kate about one who sounded (at least to Kate) eminently suitable, Dolly sounded bored.

It occurred to Kate just then that it was Dolly, not she, who had been the loser, had been the unfortunate object of their father's obsessive love. He had left her a legacy of his two broken marriages, disastrous love affairs, frustrations. And then he had left her the means to get all of these things for herself. Dolly needed only to sit and be adored, like their mother, beautiful and, now, rich. Perhaps that was really the reason that Kate did not resent his leaving everything but the house to Dolly. Kate had always thought of herself as the prisoner of this house; but wasn't Dolly a prisoner of the wider world? Had her freedom been bought with a fence around it?

At least she had her television work to steady her, although perhaps it offered Dolly too much celebrity for her own good.

In that little role of hers, Dolly had probably entered into the fantasies of most of the men in London.

PART III

Garden Wall

14

〜✥〜

T HE parlor of Stella Broome's terraced house had a view across the
street of a launderette and a Chinese restaurant and take-away
called Mr. Wong and Son.

Jury sat on one of a pair of armchairs slipcovered in a design of fading
chrysanthemums; the rug was garlanded in the center and the corners with
roses; the wallpaper was an endless repetition of pagodas, Roman columns,
and hanging gardens down whose walls trailed roses and wisteria. The
apron that Stella Broome wore was patterned with camellias, and the
ashtray she held in her lap gave off a woodsy odor.

She had, he suspected, the beginnings of emphysema, given the way she
hacked when she inhaled. He was glad Wiggins wasn't here to see her light
one cigarette from the stub of another. She was a woman in her fifties,
overweight and careless of her looks. Her face was round and the skin
tight and slightly waxy, reflecting the camellia pattern of the apron.

It was depressing, this dead garden of a room, and as if to emphasize the
fact that nothing moved or breathed, there were vases spotted here and
there on tables and mantel filled with either plastic or paper or dried
flowers.

Stella Broome had been talking about the death of her daughter: "I told
her, didn't I? I told her she'd get into trouble, hitching rides like she did.
But she wouldn't listen, not her." She shook her head and reclaimed her
glass of sherry.

That she talked about the death as if it were an infraction of parental
discipline suggested to Jury an attempt to bury the fact, to draw her
daughter back—late perhaps, drunk perhaps, but back.

"No, I can't help. All I know is Sheila left here in the morning for work
and said she'd got a ride to Bristol."

"From all we've found, she didn't seem to know anyone there," said Jury.

"Oh, that'd make no odds to Sheila. She just wanted to get away. She was always wanting to get away." Stella Broome poured another glass of sherry, pulled a tissue from the box beside a silver-framed photograph of Sheila.

"What about her friends, Mrs. Broome? The fellow she was going about with, for instance."

"I've told all this to police before. That commander or whatever he calls himself—"

"Divisional commander." Jury had to smile. From the way she spoke, Macalvie might have been pulling ranks out of a hat.

"Whatever. Harassment, that's what I call it." She lit another cigarette.

"Divisional Commander Macalvie is very thorough. And sometimes that might seem like harassment—" And sometimes is, he thought. "—but witnesses have been known to forget details that can come out if questions are asked over again." Especially if they're lying first time around. Though Jury didn't think the mother was lying, necessarily.

"Maybe," she said. She sounded doubtful. "Well, there's Gerald, Gerald Fox. That was her young man, such as he is." She sniffed. "Though I will say he was cut up over her—" Stella Broome pressed the wadded tissue to her mouth to forestall a bout of tears.

It could have been that glassful of sherry, he thought, but perhaps that merely helped release bottled-up feelings. He wondered if the flowery sentiments of the room were not some unconscious desire to express emotions she otherwise repressed. He thought Stella Broome probably prided herself on toughness. Her life must have been lonely; perhaps she had to marshal all of her forces in order to defend herself against this new onslaught. Hence the carping criticism.

"I wonder if I could have a little of that sherry?" asked Jury. It might afford her a bit of companionship. He filled her glass and went to the kitchen for another one. It gave her a few minutes to weep without being stared at by Scotland Yard.

"Thank you." She blew her nose. "Don't know what came over me."

"You should let go more, Mrs. Broome." Inwardly, he smiled. He sounded like Wiggins. He asked again about Gerald Fox, feeling it was merely repetitive; Macalvie would have covered that ground thoroughly.

"Yes, well, he was devoted to Sheila and she treated him like he wasn't worth nothing. Felt sorry for him sometimes, I did. That's the only reason she went up to London—to make him jealous. Oh, I knew it was probably all lies, the men she said she went out with. An old man with plenty of money, used to call him her Sugar Daddy—that was one. She said he'd come round to the flat to pick her up in his fancy car. If that ain't something! Then there was a dancer in some West End musical, fairy I'd bet; and—"

Jury interrupted. "Did she ever mention any names?"

"Guy-somebody. That was the dancer. Had a fancy car, some foreign make. Anyone had a flash car Sheila'd just swoon over. Flash cars and flash men, that was Sheila's style. Well, she didn't have a license herself; I mean, they took it away from her for drink-driving. Far as I'm concerned, they should. Too much drinking these days, anyway." Mournfully, she looked at her glass. Perhaps she was thinking she hadn't set the best example; that she might have nudged Sheila off the straight and narrow herself. "If I'd of got married again, maybe Sheila wouldn't have been so wild. It needs a man to straighten out a girl like that. All those men she said courted her—"

Stella Broome pressed her fingertips to her forehead as if remembering gave her a headache. Finally, she shook her head. "All I know is Sheila'd talk and talk about these fellas, probably to Gerald, too, to make him jealous. I don't even know she was telling the truth. Why'd any rich man dance attendance on Sheila?"

Jury looked at the photograph sitting next to the sherry bottle. "She was very pretty." Pretty, in a tartish way, he thought. Too much makeup, bleached hair. What had Macalvie said—"bottled-in-blond"? Jury frowned. "You said something about an older man. What about him?"

"Him? Well, I don't know, exactly. When she'd start in like that, I'd just stop listening, sometimes. All those men she claimed she'd got on a string." Her forehead creased with the effort of thinking and she stopped rocking suddenly. "That lorry driver that picked her up. They let him go." Stella Broome wadded the handkerchief under her nose again and shivered.

"A waitress at the Little Chef saw her get out of the cab, and the artic pull away. Commander Macalvie was satisfied he had nothing to do with it."

"Well, it's past now. I don't know why police are raking it over again. It was some psycho picked her up. Some psycho."

"Yes, that's perfectly possible. But I'll tell you why we're raking it up, Mrs. Broome. There was a woman killed in London, killed the same way your daughter was, with her own scarf."

She stopped rocking suddenly. "Oh, dear. Oh, that's terrible. You think it was the same person?"

"Because of the—method, it's just possible."

"But then it must be like I said. Some crazy."

"Did your daughter ever mention a David?"

"Not that I remember." She had taken another plunge or two into the sherry bottle; by now she was on her fourth or fifth. The words slurred slightly as she said, "Don't think she ever said that name." Stella seemed to be studying the wallpaper over Jury's shoulder; taking an imaginary walk through her botanical gardens, perhaps.

He waited for a moment to see if anything would occur to her. But she appeared to be rocking—and drinking—herself to sleep. Her head nodded like a flower on its stem. He got up and said, "Well, I'll be leaving now, Mrs. Broome. If you remember anything, anything at all, you'll get in touch, won't you?"

Her head snapped up and she shook herself. "Yes." She got up with considerable effort, steadying herself on the arm of the sofa. "But I ain't calling *him,* that commander or whoever he is." On their way to the door, she plucked the dried flowers from the table and ran her fingers over them, dusting them. "Where'll you be?"

Jury handed her a card. "New Scotland Yard. Just call this number, Mrs. Broome."

Now she seemed as reluctant to let him go as she had first been to have him stay. She kept looking and looking at the card as if it might be a lucky souvenir.

He did not like leaving her alone, but he couldn't stop here all day. And anyway there would always be another day to be faced. Jury looked round the room, at the dried bouquets, the walled gardens. A fragment of a poem came to him . . . *Be still, the hanging gardens are a dream . . . that over Persian roses blew to kiss. . . .* What had "kiss" rhymed with? He could not remember where the lines came from or for whom the kiss was meant. A queen, he thought. What Sheila Broome had wanted to be, perhaps.

"I like your wallpaper. It's very . . . pretty," he added lamely, unable to find a proper word. "Good-bye, Mrs. Broome. Don't forget to call. You've been very helpful."

On the pavement, he looked back. She was still there, clutching the fake bouquet. He wondered if the younger Stella had clutched her bridal bouquet that way. Probably she had forgotten the happiness of such a day. And Sheila would never experience it.

Sergeant Wiggins was sitting in Macalvie's office drinking a cup of tea when Jury walked in.

"Where is he?" Jury nodded at the desk as big as a lake and afloat beneath a pile of papers, pens, and files.

"Forensics lab," said Wiggins. "To see someone named Thwaite." He sniffed and drew out his snowdrift of a handkerchief. "Only glad I'm not Thwaite."

"That makes two of us." Jury smiled and nodded toward the door. "Come on, let's go look for him."

A uniformed police constable directed them to the lab, which lay at the end of a confusion of corridors.

Once through the swinging doors to the last corridor, the directions became superfluous. Jury simply followed the sound of a voice, which finally gave way to an onslaught of invectives as they came nearer.

It wasn't a *him,* Jury saw, as he looked through the glass square set in the door. The woman barely came up to Macalvie's shoulder, but she was reaching for somewhere around the temples, given the way she was handling the microscope.

Macalvie, although not inordinately large, managed to gain six inches in height and girth by arranging himself like a cliffside in front of this object of his displeasure, whom Jury assumed to be Sergeant Thwaite. Given the tension in the room, any knock would probably have ricocheted off the door, so Jury simply pulled it open to hear the divisional commander going on about the ax.

Or Exe, as Jury now deciphered it.

". . . stand there and tell me all day, Gilly. We pulled him outta the Exe, but he wasn't *in* the effing Exe when he died—" Macalvie turned a fraction, caught sight of Jury, nodded by way of indifferent greeting, and returned to his argument.

"If I could just have that back now," said Gilly Thwaite, reaching for the microscope that Macalvie had wrested from her. "Do you think that specimen is going to stand up and salute?"

"You're not forensics, Gilly."

"Neither are you," she snapped.

Jury gave Thwaite a gold star for courage. She had brown curls as tight as springs and smoky gray eyes, the smoke no doubt funneling up from the fires within. One arm leaned on the black marble of the lab table, the hand fisted as if she could hardly wait to slug him. When she opened her mouth, Macalvie looked at it like a dentist with a drill.

He turned to Jury. "Let's get out of here; I need a drink," he said, pulling Wiggins along with him less by the hand on his shoulder than by the air sucked into any vacuum the D.C. left in his wake. He turned back to Sergeant Thwaite. "Would you just let Waliman do his job? Such as he is," Macalvie added sotto voce.

Gilly Thwaite, back to her microscope, looked up. "You'll just have to carry on without me."

"What a mouth. If she parked her tongue, it'd be on a yellow line," said Macalvie.

The pub was in the old part of Exeter in one of the Tudor buildings surrounding the cathedral green. The short trip in the police Cortina, with Macalvie cannoning from curb to curb around old Exeter's confines, was filled with various complaints and imprecations—he hadn't eaten in two days (Jury could believe it); he was going to quit and take off for America (Jury didn't believe it) and get a private license (ditto). "You've seen *The Maltese Falcon* once too often, Macalvie," said Jury as they pushed open the door of the Black Swan.

Macalvie peered through the glass-surround of the steam table and asked the girl to serve up a plate of cottage pie, sausages, peas, and bread. He inspected the plate to see if there was any more room, then said, "You guys want anything? They do good bar meals."

Jury shook his head; Wiggins asked the girl for a cheese toastie. Then, looking at Macalvie's piled-up plate, Wiggins shook his head. "Roughage, you need. Lettuce. You're probably like him." Wiggins nodded toward Jury. "Don't eat right for days and try to make up for it all in one go, and stuff yourself with the wrong things."

"You call a cheese toastie a *right* thing?" Still, he looked doubtfully at his plate and handed it back for some salad. Jury went to the other end of the bar for the drinks, thinking they must have some common ancestor. Macalvie, who took advice from no one but the archangel Gabriel, often took Wiggins's dissertations on health with more than a grain of salt.

It was salt they were arguing over when Jury sat down at the table. "Hypertension, hell." He snowed his cottage pie under with a half-dozen shakes. "So what happened with Stella Broome?" Macalvie made a little pool in the center of his potatoes.

"Nothing that you don't already know, I imagine. She talked about Sheila's boyfriends, a Gerald Fox, Guy somebody, others nameless. Unfortunately, Stella often tuned her out. What about this older man, the one Sheila called her Sugar Daddy?"

"That's a nil, Jury. Oh, there apparently *was* some old guy—old meaning twice her age. I chatted up Vera, the one she used to visit, about him. Too bad Vera didn't much care for Sheila, said she was a freeloader, and didn't pay a hell of a lot of attention to what she said either. But she did catch a glimpse of him standing beside his car. One of those Jag XJ6s. You know, the kind with the fourteen interchangeable roofs they issue cops like us. But we couldn't trace the guy."

Macalvie shook his head, poured on more salt. "It's all in the files. We talked to two, three hundred people. Relatives, relatives of relatives. Friends, friends of friends. Nothing."

Wiggins was depositing two or three drops of a neon-yellow fluid in his lager. "Couldn't this lorry driver, Riley, have picked her up later—?"

Macalvie was fascinated, watching the descent of the drops as he said, "It wasn't the driver. There wasn't the sign of any lorry parked in that woods. . . . Wiggins, what is that stuff?"

The lager had taken on an alien color. "Got something in my chest." He coughed and hit his chest with his fisted hand.

"Probably a Martian," said Macalvie, as he went back to his sausages. "The waitress said he set Sheila down at the edge of the road just after they left the Little Chef. The Higgins dame certainly wasn't lying and she seemed to be very observant. Though she couldn't identify the picture of David Marr we showed her. I mean, couldn't say yes or no, definitely. Just that he looked 'familiar.' That's something to go on. Only the constable I had go in there and grab a coffee, he's tall and dark like Marr—he looked 'familiar' too. I think she was trying too hard to be helpful."

Wiggins was following up the yellow drops with a small white envelope filled with pink crystals that he tapped into the lager. "It's just that you seem determined it was someone who knew Sheila. That silence inside the cafe sounds like maybe they'd been fighting and it flared up again when she got in the cab." He drank the lager, which had turned a turgid shade of pinkish yellow.

"What condition have you got, Wiggins, the Black Death? Yes, they knew each other, I still say they knew each other."

"The scarf doesn't suggest premeditation to me, Macalvie. It sounds spur of the moment."

Macalvie shrugged. "Not if he knew she always wore one. Most women do. Anyway, you think he couldn't have been carrying something else? Knife? Gun?"

Jury shook his head. "As I said, it could have been that Sheila just walked into the wrong place at the wrong time."

"You make it sound like Fate, Jury. I don't believe in star-crossed paths."

"It happens."

"Not in Devon." Macalvie smiled.

15

❦

THE house itself had no name. Through the twilit snow, Jury's lights picked out only a small bronze plaque bearing the single word *Winslow*, set in a stone pillar at the end of the curving drive. For a few moments he sat in the car, smoking and looking through the small wood where fallen branches and rotting logs showed the groundskeeper—if there was one—was anywhere but in the grounds. He slammed the door of the Ford, sending a small landslide of snow from the bonnet of the car to the ground.

Jury pulled at the bell and looked up at the straight gray face of the house. He would not have chosen it as a sanctuary from London, although it was certainly quiet enough. "Desolate" would be a better word, he thought. Perhaps it was that, really, that added to its baronial splendor.

A rustic-looking man, his face fretted with the tiny lines of the excessive drinker, opened the door and stuck his head around it, scanning Jury's person with suspicion that only increased when Jury showed him his warrant card and said he was here to see Mrs. Winslow.

The man opened the door farther and beckoned with his hand as if he were trying to pull the malingerer on the step inside. "Coom on in; I'll tell 'em." No proper butler, certainly; probably the absentee groundsman or gardener.

The hall was large and cold and added to the impression of baronial splendor, with the array of armaments on one wall, the niches on the other into which plaster busts of saints or gods had been set. A central staircase of highly polished mahogany climbed up to a galleried first floor. He walked to the newel post and looked up; the picture Plant had mentioned on the telephone showed a blond young woman and a little girl of perhaps seven or eight.

On each side of the front door, an arched window gave a narrow view of the woodland. Snow drifted slowly down, masking the black beeches and yews. They looked more like shadows of trees. It turned his mind toward the Bristol road, the wood in which Sheila Broome had been found. He frowned slightly; something bothered him, something he had heard about Sheila Broome, a tiny print left on his mind much like the dark and delicate tracks of the birds. A missal thrush landed and rocked a thin branch of the nearest beechwood; small clumps of snow sifted down.

"Sorry, Superintendent, for keeping you waiting."

It was David Marr. Jury had not heard him coming and was momentarily disoriented from staring out at the hypnotic scene.

Marr smiled slightly. "We've met."

"I know." Jury also smiled. "I think I was a little mesmerized by your wood. I like the snow."

Marr raised his eyebrows in mock surprise. "You go out in it, do you?"

"Occasionally. I'm a little late because of the roads."

They were walking toward a double door to the right of the hall. "Don't apologize. We're the ones who kept *you* waiting. John isn't really much of a butler. Not much of a groundskeeper, either, come to think of it. We're in the drawing room here, all properly arranged for your questions."

~~~~~

Properly arranged was what the Winslows were. It was masterly, in a way; they stood or sat rather like actors who had just been blocked and who had now left off wrestling with their scripts. Marion Winslow, wearing a black velvet lounge-robe, sat in a high-backed mahogany armchair pulled out several feet from a huge marble fireplace. A Christmas tree, undecorated except for strings of unlit lights and a tiny, spun-glass angel on top, stood rather gloomily to the right of the mantel. Edward Winslow stood in front of the fireplace, smoking. David Marr lent the casual touch, just the right touch to make it all convincing, impromptu, as he fixed Jury and himself a whiskey and water. In the positions of Marion Winslow and her son, there was almost an imitation of the pose in the portrait directly above the overmantel, yet it did not seem at all to be a self-conscious posing. After handing Jury his drink, David sat down on a fine Queene Anne sofa, his legs stretched out before him.

Jury intended to talk with each of them separately, but not right now. He did not want to break up this family gathering; it was interesting.

They talked for a few moments politely about the condition of the roads and the unexpected snowfall, while Jury lit a cigarette and let his eye stray to the circular claw-footed table near him that held a collection of photographs, some small, some large; simply or elaborately framed. When the talk had died down like the slowly drifting snow, Jury reached for a small picture in a chased silver frame of the child in the painting on the landing. She was very pretty, with large liquid eyes and pale hair. His little sister looked, Jury thought, as Edward Winslow might have looked at that age.

Jury noticed that Marion Winslow was watching, tracking the movement of frame from table to chair and back again. "That was my daughter, Phoebe." Her voice was pleasantly low, but as flat and calm and cold as the wintry landscape he had passed through on the road from Exeter.

"I heard about the accident. I'm sorry."

She gave a slight nod; her brother had risen to replenish his glass and now stood, hand in pocket of jacket, looking down abstractedly at the fire. Then he turned, as if to say something, but it was Edward who spoke: "I was very fond of Phoebe." He sighed. "Well, we all were." He moved closer to his mother's chair and laid a hand on her shoulder. She seemed to be looking off at blankness.

Jury wondered about the black dress. The child had died over two years ago, not, certainly, a long time. Like yesterday as far as grieving was concerned; but for the clothes of mourning, a little long. Though Jury doubted that Marion Winslow meant anything like this by the simple, elegantly cut black gown.

"Look, the family album is fascinating," said David, reclaiming his seat on the sofa, "but have you turned up anything that'll let me off the hook?"

Jury felt rather sorry for Marr despite the callous comment about the family album. Put aside the circumstantial and there was no evidence to say he had killed Ivy Childess. But there was the circumstantial, nonetheless. "I'm afraid nothing conclusive, Mr. Marr."

"Hell, let's settle for something *in*conclusive."

Jury smiled, but shook his head. He was glad that the subject had been introduced by one of them. "It would be helpful if I could talk with you alone, Mr. Marr. As a matter of fact—"

This was interrupted by Marr's saying, "You've already talked with me alone, Superintendent."

"I was just saying, I'd really like to talk with each of you alone. If that wouldn't be too inconvenient."

He was a little surprised when Marion Winslow laughed. "Somehow I think we'll find the time, Mr. Jury." She rose from her chair and with Edward, left the room.

"This is getting to be the highlight of my day," said David, splashing more whiskey into his glass, then holding up the decanter and looking at Jury.

Jury shook his head. "I'm glad we're not boring you."

"Not at all, not at all. How many ways are there to inquire into a telephone call. At least now, you can ask my sister in person."

"I was wondering, Mr. Marr, if you've ever been in Exeter?"

David Marr looked up from his drink, surprised. "Well! Here's a new approach." He leaned his head against the back of the sofa. "Exeter, Exeter, Exeter. Yes, a long time ago. Took a turn round the cathedral. Then round the pubs."

"How long a time ago?"

David shrugged. "Ten years, perhaps." He looked at Jury. "I can see a whole new line of questioning's opened up. What happened in Exeter?"

"Sheila Broome. You didn't happen to know—?"

"Never heard of her." His answer was quick, tangling with the end of Jury's question. "And that 'didn't' suggests something's happened to her." He turned his gaze ceilingward again. "Good God." He sighed. "I *do* hope the next question isn't going to be 'Where were you on the night of—?' "

Jury smiled. "Twenty-nine February."

Marr turned quickly to look at him. "That's ten *months* ago, Superintendent."

"I know."

"Although the dates of my tumultuous affairs with young ladies are seared into my brain, I honestly cannot remember that particular one. Sheila, you say?"

"Broome. That's too bad. When you've a bit of spare time, try."

David groaned. "Are you going to tell me, Superintendent, that *another* woman has had her life snuffed out? Snuffed, you apparently think, by me?" He slipped farther down into the sofa and rolled the cool glass across his forehead.

"No, I wasn't going to tell you that." Jury sat forward. "David, for someone in your position, don't you think you're being a little glib?"

"Thank you. But my position happens to be that I hadn't one damned thing to do with the death of Ivy. Or anyone else." He drank off his whiskey and stared morosely at the fire.

"Okay. I'd like to talk with Edward."

David turned, surprised. "You mean that's *all,* Superintendent? I was certain you were going to grind me to powder. Well, I'd be gleeful about this, but it bodes ill: you haven't even come up with something or someone more interesting than I. And I doubt I'm much fun anymore."

"I'll keep trying."

No painting or photograph could really do Edward Winslow credit. The snapshot Jury had just returned to David Marr only hinted at his nephew's good looks, probably because a camera couldn't capture the grace with which he moved. Yet, Jury thought that the portraitist had taken the aristocratic bones and bearing too seriously, for though Edward was both handsome and elegant he was also offhand, as if his manner, unlike his clothes, had been pulled off the rack. A designer of men's couture would love to see him in ascot or reefer; Edward himself preferred the wool sweater and collar open at the neck.

He walked into the room with a sort of shamble and an uncertain smile. Then he settled into the corner of the sofa that David had just vacated, and propped his head against his hand. "If you don't mind my saying so, this is all rather strange—I mean, that Scotland Yard would come to Somers Abbas. Oh, sorry . . ." Edward colored a bit, as if thinking that inquiry into Scotland Yard's *own* inquiry were poor form.

Did they all, thought Jury, think of it as a game? Cricket? "You divide your time between Somers Abbas and London, is that right?" asked Jury. When he nodded, Jury asked, "Any particular reason you live here rather than there?"

Edward laughed. "You sound like Mother. Mother says she doesn't want me hanging about, propping her up."

"Your mother doesn't seem in much need of propping, Mr. Winslow."

Edward got up, as David had done, and fixed himself a whiskey, but a very small one. "She does." He drank it off, neat. "Though she hides it pretty well, she does. Since my sister died, mother's been pretty—withdrawn. She—Phoebe—was hit by a car; she dashed right in front of the car; he didn't see her until he was nearly on top of her. Or so he said. It wasn't technically a hit-and-run, since the chap apparently stopped at a call box three blocks away and called police." He looked sadly at Jury. "But I found Phoebe; Hugh was in the house." He paused. "He ran out later."

Jury nodded but said nothing, as he watched Ned Winslow walk about, stopping at the spruce to retrieve the spun-glass angel that winked in the light as he repositioned it on its top branch. Since Ned Winslow had been there—*How did she look? What was she wearing? Did she speak at all?*—he was perhaps doomed to carry the burden, like a tribal memory.

"I'm sorry," said Jury. "Your uncle mentioned you were a poet, a published one, at that. You must be very good."

He laughed. "Well, I suppose you're right—I mean about publication being coincidental with one's worth. And writing poetry certainly doesn't seem like much to be doing, especially to someone on the dole."

"I was wondering," said Jury, "why you go to the expense of keeping a flat in Belgravia when you've the house in Knightsbridge."

"That's simple. My father lives there." He looked at Jury. "I don't get on with him." Ned leaned forward to poke at the fire. A log split and crumbled and a saw-edge of bluish flame spurted up, casting a web of shadow across his face. The color of his eyes, when he looked over at Jury, shifted like cornelian from brown to gold.

"When your uncle called on Monday night, were you here?" Jury watched Ned Winslow, who did not answer immediately.

"No."

"But your mother told you about the call."

"Oh, certainly. After all, it's about the only thing keeping David out of the dock, isn't it?"

Marion Winslow did not take her eyes from Jury as she went to the high-backed armchair.

Neither did Jury move; he kept to the chair beside the center table nearly ten feet away, across the expanse of Kirman carpet.

Her hands rested on the ends of the mahogany armrests; her legs were crossed, a wave of black velvet over the tips of her shoes. She wore no jewelry and little if any makeup. She did not seem to go in for ornaments.

"There's really nothing I can add to what I've already told you, Superintendent. Though I certainly don't mind telling you again." She smiled coolly. "It's the telephone call I imagine you're most interested in?"

"One of the things, yes."

"David rang up, I'd say, close to eleven on the Monday night."

"And you can't fix the time more precisely?"

"No. I'm sorry. Sometimes my husband's answering machine picks up calls and it asks the time. If I'm out of earshot and the servants aren't around, I set it. But that night, I was in the library, reading." She thought for a moment. "I'd say between ten forty-five and eleven or a few minutes past."

"A bit late to call."

She laughed. "Not for David. Not here."

"What did he expect of you?"

With a little smile, she said, "Money. And I suppose a shoulder to cry on. I told you: he'd just walked out on Ivy Childess; he got weary of her nagging about marrying."

"Hadn't he ever intended to marry her?"

"I doubt it very seriously."

"Your brother just doesn't fancy marriage in general?"

She shook her head. "No, in particular. Particularly, Ivy Childess."

"You knew her?"

Her eyebrows arched in mild surprise. "No. I'd *met* her. There's a difference. It was at our house in London. We had some friends round for drinks. My son and brother were there. And David brought Ivy." She shrugged and added: "And Lucinda St. Clair, I remember."

"St. Clair."

"Yes. They live at the north edge of Somers Abbas. A rather rococo house which they've named 'The Steeples.' Lucinda is the older daughter, and we've known her for a long time." Marion rested her head against the tall back of the chair and looked up at the ceiling. "Actually, I think you might want to talk with Lucinda; she's extremely fond of David." She reached out and plucked up a small notebook and gold pencil and wrote rapidly. "Understand, I'm not suggesting Lucinda will give you an unbiased account. Here's the telephone number and address. Though anyone in the village can tell you where the St. Clairs live." She tore out the page and placed it on the table. They were too far apart for reaching.

Marion Winslow was a purposeful woman, thought Jury. No words wasted, no movement embellished. She was, he thought, rather like a fisherman. Everything weighed and measured before thought became act. She gently pulled in the line, took up the slack. "By 'extremely fond' do you mean she's in love with him?"

She nodded. "Yes, and it's too bad. David doesn't return the feeling." Looking again at the fire-shadows on the ceiling, she added, but as if it were of no consequence, "I like Lucinda."

"You're pretty much your brother's confidante, then?"

Again, she nodded. "That's why I wasn't at all surprised when he called late Monday."

"You said you talked for about twenty minutes. Can you be more exact?"

"No. Twenty minutes to half an hour."

That would put Marr in his apartment from approximately ten-fifty to eleven-ten or -twenty, if he left the pub just on quarter to eleven, and *if* it took him Wiggins's estimate of ten minutes to walk to Shepherd Market. The better part of the time allowed for Ivy Childess's murder. No airtight alibi, but better than nothing. He could certainly have walked *back* to the Running Footman, strangled her, and returned to Shepherd Market within the twenty minutes between the pub's closing and the woman's passing with her dog. Twenty minutes, difficult. Thirty, easy. That extra ten minutes could make all the difference. But there would, in that case, remain the problem of why Ivy would have hung about Hays Mews for twenty minutes.

"Your husband spends most of his time in London, does he?" asked Jury mildly.

Marion flinched. "Yes, he does."

"But you yourself don't go to London often?"

"No."

"Mr. Winslow keeps a sort of office here, does he?"

"Yes. He's a financial consultant; I imagine he needs to keep in touch."

Jury thought that "imagine" defined the Winslows' relationship. Marion and Hugh were certainly not one another's confidant. But he asked, anyway, "And did your husband dislike Ivy Childess?"

"I don't remember his ever saying anything about her. One way or another." She shrugged.

"Your husband spends most of his time in London, doesn't he?"

"Yes."

"Though he comes here seldom, does he come—well, regularly?"

"No. Irregularly."

"And you, do you stay at your house there?"

She seemed to be thinking. "Rarely. More often at Claridge's. I wouldn't go at all except to see Ned and David. I don't want always to be dragging them down here."

Jury smiled. "If ever two men didn't look as if they'd been 'dragged' I'd say it was David and Ned."

"Thank you. That sounded like a compliment." She seemed to be studying her hands. "You see—and I'm sure you can understand—I dislike the house in Knightsbridge intensely." She looked up. "Phoebe died there." Her glance shifted from Jury to the table beside him holding the framed photographs.

"I can understand, yes." His look followed her own, straying to the center table. There was a photo in an old-fashioned walnut frame of a small girl, smiling, strands of light hair blowing across her face. Jury studied it. "I noticed there's a painting, a portrait on the landing upstairs. Is it of her?"

"Yes. Phoebe and Rose." She looked away. "Rose was Edward's wife. She left. I wish he'd marry again; perhaps he'd have better luck. How anyone could marry Ned for money is beyond me. But she did; she managed to clean out the account before she left without a word. Yet it's David, not Ned, who hates that portrait. He keeps telling me to take it down. But it's the only one we have of Phoebe, and one doesn't go cutting people out of portraits, does one?"

But one does cut people out of wills, he thought. "You said your brother wanted money. A lot?"

She laughed. "He always does. David's frightfully spendthrift. How he could go through the money he has in the last few years, I can't imagine."

"What about the family fortune? Who inherits what?"

"It's divided evenly, among the three of us. It's about, oh, five million, I expect." She shrugged it off as if it were five pounds. "There is a codicil, though: David inherits when he marries. Our father thought he would run through his share in a year if he hadn't a wife to talk some sense into him."

There was a glint of victory in her eyes. "So he'd have every reason to keep Ivy Childess alive, wouldn't he?"

His eye was caught by another photo that looked like an enlargement of the same snapshot he had borrowed from Marr's flat. David and Edward caught suddenly in a moment of laughter. They were wearing tennis sweaters, and Ned's hand held tightly to the handle of a racquet that disappeared over his shoulder. From the position of both Jury guessed they must have had their arms about one another's shoulders. One had won, one had lost, both were happy.

"Edward is very fond of David, isn't he?"

"Extremely. *And,* believe it or not, so is David of Edward."

Jury replaced the photo. "Why 'believe it or not'?"

"Only because David so loves to adopt that cynical air. Don't you believe it."

"I don't."

"Because he's got a passionate enough nature to do murder?"

"I didn't mean that."

Jury replaced the photograph; she picked up the bit of notebook paper; a silence fell. He felt somehow awkward, sitting here drinking the dregs of his whiskey—he felt a chump, actually, but didn't know why. He looked from his glass to the silky surface of a Belgian tapestry that seemed to ripple in the light from the high windows like the crests of incoming waves. Through the twilit panes he saw the snow had stopped. The beeches stood in a dark column, but now they were ash-brown. Screened by snow they had looked black. The surface of things could be deceptive.

"Mr. Jury?"

Jury looked up. She had gone to the window to fasten the catch and pull the heavy curtains together, almost as if she hadn't wanted him to see this metamorphosis at dusk. Her head was tilted slightly as if she were trying to see his eyes. "Sorry. I suppose I was woolgathering."

She smiled. "Don't apologize. I do it all the time."

Her attempt to seem at ease was very studied, he thought.

"I'm not trying to get away from you. But I just thought perhaps you had no more questions."

"You're right, none." Standing before the window, her hands lightly laced before her and with her very dark hair and pale complexion, Marion Winslow gave the impression of one whom great misfortune had made very quiet but very sure. Capable, perhaps, of nearly anything. Lying would come easily to her to protect someone, because the old rules no longer applied, the moral element had shifted like sand. He had risen too, of course, and said, "Thank you very much, Mrs. Winslow. I would like to have a look round, if you don't mind."

She nodded. "I'll send Ned along to show you whatever you want to see."

He returned the nod. As she walked in those clothes of mourning, her back straight, across to the door, he thought that Marion Winslow was a woman upon whom society could no longer intrude. She had locked the windows, drawn the curtains, shut the door.

16

THE gallows sign of the Mortal Man creaked eerily in the wind and the snow, lit by a dull metal lamp that lent its sickle-curve of light to the mortality of the sallow-faced figure in the sign. The light spilling from the windows of the inn's public bar was no brighter, no more cheerful. It crept round the edges and through the slits of a boarded-up window, whose shutters banged as fretfully as did the sign. No matter that during the day, the Mortal Man must have belonged to the pretty picture cut by the village green, the duckpond, the row of thatched-roof cottages beyond—here, in the dark and the cold it looked vacant, transient, divested of an inn's life and good cheer.

Inside, this impression was quickly dispelled. There was surely enough life to go round the green and back several times over. A cacophony of shouting voices met him—or rather, blasted past him, in the person of a woman, a youngish girl, a younger boy with a dog. The dog stopped when he saw Jury, as smartly as if he'd run into a wall, ran madly three times around Jury's legs, and continued, yapping, after the boy.

In another minute, this happy quartet rushed back from the other direction, apparently not having solved their logistical problem, if that were the problem. The dog remembered to run around Jury's legs again, in some sort of magical incantation, before it zipped off after the others.

"The common form of greeting at the Mortal Man," said Melrose Plant, who appeared in the doorway of the public bar, smiling broadly, smoking one of his small cigars. "They'll be back; you escaped serious damage this time, but don't press your luck." Plant motioned him in. "The St. Clairs have saved you, possibly, a trip to the Steeples. Count yourself twice fortunate."

Behind the bar, the burly owner appeared to be comparing notes with a tall man who sat with three glasses before him at a nearby table. He was introduced to Jury as St. John St. Clair, and the young woman next to him as the daughter, Lucinda. The gentleman behind the bar, who was slapping his bar towel around, apparently on the track of a fly, snapped it so smartly at the mirror that a patch of the gilt frame fell off.

Jury's offer to stand drinks was met with a sad headshake by St. Clair. He had tried, he said, studying the three glasses before him, all of the Warboyses' stock of Irish whiskey. They had been found wanting. This was, of course, no reflection on Mr. Warboys but on the general instability of that country. The chief difference between the innkeeper and his unhappy guest was that one had a round, red face; the other, a sad, long one. For both, Armageddon was drawing near.

Nathan Warboys lost no time in trying to persuade Jury that, if he had any plans for marrying, he should drop them immediately. "Take my Sally. I mean, I mean, don't think I don't know what that 'un's always on about. Out she goes, every night, dressed like a dog's dinner."

Apparently, the hound had taken this as a call to the front, for he streaked across the room and grabbed St. Clair's walking stick between his teeth with an almighty growl. As he pulled and growled, the handle caught on the narrow table leg, sending table and drinks spilling about. Nathan Warboys picked up a piece of the wood stacked against the counter and let it fly, barely missing Melrose's head, then said someone would be in to mop up the mess.

Melrose hoped not. St. Clair took it quite philosophically, dabbing at his shirt and picking up the conversation where Nathan had dropped it. "You are right, of course, Mr. Warboys. Marriage can be an extremely sad affair, though I can't agree it is the fault of the woman. No, it is the fault of everybody. Certainly, there *are* wives—not yours, not mine, at least not yet —who do cause the most dreadful trouble. Why, look at poor Marion—"

"Marion's never caused any trouble, Daddy."

"*She* hasn't, no. We know of no trouble at all *she's* caused. The fact Hugh stays away must be owing to something else, but we don't want to talk about that. They don't make cloth like they used to; I doubt this stain will come out." He patted his tie with the bar towel. "I'm speaking of that person that poor David is accused of murdering. What a perfectly dreadful mess."

"Did you know her, Mr. St. Clair?" asked Jury.

Nathan Warboys topped up his glass and said, "You want to stay away from them kind, you do."

"No, I didn't. Fortunately. Though I believe Lucinda did."

When Jury turned to her, Lucinda said, "I met her once, Ivy Childess. I hardly knew her. It was at a little party in Knightsbridge." Eagerly, she leaned toward Jury and said, "David couldn't *possibly* have done that. It's just not in his nature to do something so—awful."

There was no question that Plant had been right about Lucinda St. Clair's attachment to David Marr. Jury wondered how far it might take her, that attachment. "Do you visit the Winslow house much, then? Do you go up to London, Miss St. Clair?"

"Hardly ever," said Lucinda.

"Best you don't, my dear," said her father. "And don't forget Edward's misfortune," St. Clair went on, his sonorous voice blending with the hollow sound of the bell in the village church tolling the hour.

Warboys, a toothpick jumping about in his mouth, said, "You mean that there wife of his, a right treat, weren't she? Just up and left and never a good-bye, and never a word since. Well, that were a long time ago, weren't it? Still, it's some way for a wife to act, just leavin' without so much's a word." Nathan then seemed to be reconsidering the merits of this unwifely behavior when his own wife appeared to shout out last calls for dinner.

The St. Clairs left; Plant and Jury walked across the hall to the dining room, while from upstairs came a series of small crashes.

"It's just a Warboys, straightening up your room," said Melrose.

～～

"You are being treated to an evening of the Warboyses in full revel." Melrose Plant repositioned his cutlery and tucked up his threadbare dinner napkin.

Jury squinted his eyes. "Never, *never* have I seen you eat a meal with a napkin under your chin."

"That's because you've never seen me dine with the Warboyses." He lifted his roll, found it rock-hard, and hit it with the handle of his knife. "There!" The roll splintered and crumbled on the plate. "The Warboyses have unleashed my taste for violence."

"Are they joining us, then?" asked Jury, who had reached down to scratch Osmond behind the ears.

"Probably." Melrose lifted the edge of the tablecloth to look at the hound, napping happily at Jury's feet. "That dog must be dead."

The dining room was more festive than usual; they were not the only occupants of the room: in a far corner sat a man and woman who had no doubt been lured in by the announcement outside that an "English dinner plus all the trimmings" awaited them. The Warboyses' idea of "traditional" probably ran more to Sainsbury fruitcake than home-made Yorkshire pudding, Melrose thought. He observed that his and Jury's companions-in-adventure were quite silent, looking at the black panes through which they could see nothing but their own reflections. Married, he assumed, and hoped he wasn't stereotyping the couple. But he wondered why married folk always seemed uncomfortable when they dined in public, as if afraid that someone would think they'd just come from a steamy assignation if they looked at each other.

A string of white lights made an arc at the top of the window; the Warboyses' stockings were nailed to the mantel. Melrose had watched Bobby Warboys going at them hell-for-leather, all the while blathering out his complaints, as if he were nailing the entire season to a tree. A small Christmas tree with tiny winking lights sat amongst some souvenirs on a shelf overhead—a flowered bottle of green glass with the legend *A Present from Wells-Next-the-Sea;* several little photos of what looked to be absent Warboyses; one live plant and one in its throes; a stuffed red fox with its one good eye trained on Melrose (the other probably having been shot out by Nathan); a bowl of plastic fruit, whose grapes, Melrose said, must have given this particular wine its special piquancy. By the dining-room door sat a cross-eyed porcelain leopard, bedecked with tinsel. All oddments culled from some jumble sale, it looked like.

"Where's our soup?" said Melrose, twisting round to stare down the kitchen door.

On cue, Mrs. Warboys charged through it with two plates of soup. Short, stout, pale, she had been turned by the kitchen catastrophe into a quivering, livid mass. She put Melrose in mind of a mad blancmange. The soup slopped up the sides of the bowls when she set it down and announced the entree selection: "Veal cutlet, toad-in-the-hole, and Bombay duck." She flicked a glance right and left to see how each of them took it.

Melrose looked at Jury who said, "Oh, go ahead."

"I'll try it, though Bombay duck is hardly my idea of your *traditional* Christmas dinner. I was thinking more along the lines of some nice, rare roast beef." He smiled so hard he thought he'd grow dimples.

"Aye, 'tis. But we're out."

"Out?"

Mrs. Warboys nodded over her shoulder in the direction of the couple at the window. "Them two's 'ad the last bit."

"But they're the only others here."

All the while keeping an eye on them, Jury smiled and sipped his wine, a bottle that Melrose had wrestled from Nathan's stock. Everything that the Warboyses owned was considered their personal treasure, from the blind-eyed fox to the indifferent wine. "Toad-in-the-hole for me, Mrs. Warboys," said Jury.

"Yessir." She smoothed out her apron and her frown and nearly curtsied. Then she clutched the tray to her bosom and tramped off, some of the steam having decompressed.

"Toad-in-the-bloody-*hole?* You'll be sorry. It's probably real."

"Haven't had any of that since my days in Good Hope."

"Isn't that the euphemism for that chilly institution you spent your childhood in? It's always sounded to me like a Siberian winter."

"It was."

Since the kitchen door worked both ways, Mrs. Warboys's exit provided for William's entrance. He sped by the table. "You seen Sally?" he asked of them, though he'd never seen Jury until that moment. No, they hadn't. "She's gone and forgot the spuds for supper." He wheeled away.

"Who's Sally?"

"Another Warboys, the woods are full of them." Melrose continued spooning up his soup.

Jury drank his wine. "Give me your impression of the Winslow family."

"I don't think David Marr has much of an alibi, to tell the truth."

"There was a call; we traced it."

"Yes, but there's also an answering machine. Not even Telecom, incredibly efficient as it is when it comes to tracking down delinquent payments, could tell you who or what answered, could it? Only that a connection was made."

Jury was silent for a minute. "And you think Marion Winslow is lying."

Melrose shrugged. "Marion, David, Edward—they'd all lie for one another."

"But if the telephone rang, someone would have heard it."

"No. The servants were gone. You know, I was thinking—" He finished his soup and laid down his spoon. "—that alibis work two ways, don't they?"

At that moment, Sally Warboys scudded across the dining room like gray clouds hurrying before a storm and carrying a brown bag full (Melrose supposed) of the dinner spuds. "Before the storm" was accurate, too, because her father rode fast on her heels, his arms windmilling, unmindful of his clientele. Sally smacked her way into the kitchen, and Nathan apparently didn't think he needed to improve upon the bedlam (a thunderous fall of pans, a rain of cutlery), for he came straight out again. A dusty-looking cat just managed to flash its way through the door and around Nathan's foot before it got mashed by one and kicked by the other. Melrose watched its lightning progress across the room and its skid to a stop by the arched doorway, where it hissed at the porcelain leopard that it had, apparently, never accepted as cousin.

"Here he comes; pretend we're deep in our soup," whispered Melrose to Jury.

Nathan Warboys wouldn't have cared anyway, since he was not a thrifty speaker and demanded no payment in the coin of someone else's comments. With his usual scowl he said, "I mean, I mean, look at 'er, would

ya? 'Ow many men you got 'ere? I says to 'er. It's a right treat, innit, and
'er out every night . . ."

Melrose tuned him out; Jury sat there all ears. Melrose wondered under
what particular slag heap of Nathan's conversation Jury expected to find
the golden nugget. Around Jury a frozen spring became a waterfall, and
Warboys was set to run like Niagara. Fortunately, the shrill *brr-brr* of the
telephone called him to his duty.

His place was taken now by Sally Warboys, who dealt the dishes round
like a card-sharp, knocking half the cutlery from the table before she
slopped off to entertain further disasters.

"You were talking about Marr's telephone call. Go on." Jury forked up
some potatoes.

"The call provides Marion Winslow with an alibi, too. The impression I
got of her was fleeting. But even that left me with the feeling that she's a
determined woman. And Edward obviously thinks so, too, loyal as he is.
Loyal as they *all* are to one another. Of course, I only saw her for a minute
on the stair." Melrose set down his wineglass and inspected his Bombay
duck, poking it here and there with his fork. After a moment he said, "Did
you notice the portrait of Edward's wife?"

Jury nodded. "Mrs. Winslow said she kept it because of Phoebe. There's
no love lost between her and the ex-wife." Jury pulled half of a sausage
from the pastry blanket.

Melrose leaned over to look at Jury's plate: "I don't see why Mrs.
Warboys had to waste the Yorkshire pudding on toad-in-the-hole."

"How you do suffer. How's your Bombay duck?"

"It walked from Bombay. You know, Rose's leaving certainly wouldn't
sit well with the Winslow family. Neither would this duck." He held up a
morsel.

"Get back to the telephone call. When did she send the servants away?"

"I calculated it must have been the day of the murder."

"But she wouldn't have known her brother would call; the servants'
leaving wouldn't have been planned because of a nonexistent telephone
call."

"Perhaps it was her intention to go to London without anyone knowing
about it. Of course, she would turn on the answering machine. She certainly wouldn't want any calls slipping through her fingers on that particular night. I mean, of course, if she hopped it to London. And since she
often uses the machine when she's in another part of the house, or napping, no one would question her not answering. Well?"

"There's the same problem, the problem of motive. Why would she kill
Ivy Childess?"

"Possibly, to protect one of them—David or Edward. That might be the
only thing that would drive her to kill anyone."

"Protect them from what, though?"

Melrose sighed. "You're no fun."

"But this is. Like the plum in the Christmas pud." He speared the other half of the sausage and held it up on the tines of his fork. "I rather like your theory, except for something rather obvious."

"I hope you're not foolhardy enough to say things like that to Commander Macalvie. 'Obvious,' indeed!"

"Take the Beedles over there for example—"

"The who?" Melrose followed the direction of Jury's gaze. The gentleman at the far table was seeing to his bill. "How'd you know their name?"

"Nathan Warboys. Weren't you listening? I've been watching them and their extended silence. Marriage can be very relaxing, I think. No demands to make clever dinner conversation, for one—"

"Why don't you settle down?" Melrose got out his cigarette case, took out a thin hand-rolled cigar, and snapped the case shut.

"I'm talking about the way things seem. Appearance can often be the truth. One needn't interpret their silence as anger or anything at all except a desire not to converse. Sheila Broome and the lorry driver, for instance. Why not assume that Sheila and the driver were acting quite naturally? The quintessential hitchhiker refusing to converse with the person who picks her up? And the telephone call that definitely *was* made, made by David, answered by Marion? And the servants going off to visit a sickbed because someone got sick on that weekend? The killer could have been a woman, yes, of course, and *could* have been Marion Winslow. But as I said, there's still motive to consider."

Melrose took from his pocket Edward Winslow's book of poetry and handed it to Jury. "He's quite good. You know, you say these two killings have one thing in common: the method. Garroted with their own scarves wound about their necks. It makes me think of Porphyria."

"Porphyria?"

"Browning's Porphyria: '. . . Then glided in Porphyria.' Her lover strangled her with her own hair."

"That's interesting. The Porphyria murders. Macalvie would like that; he's big on repeat killings." Jury checked his watch. "I'm due at the Winslows in a little while and then back to London. Come to London, why don't you?"

Melrose shook his head. "No, I don't think so." He held up one of the two small photographs lying on the table, put that down, held up the other. He held it at arm's length, drew it forward, held it out again. He scratched his head, grimacing. "That waitress at the Little Chef. Exactly what did she say when you showed her the newspaper clipping of David Marr?"

"It was Macalvie showed her. Mary Higgins said he—David, that is—looked familiar. So Macalvie had a good-looking dark-haired cop go in for a coffee, a man about the same height and build as Marr, and she said he looked familiar, too. Macalvie thinks she was trying too hard."

Melrose picked up the picture of the Winslow family again. "It seems strange, though, this Little Chef business."

"Strange, how?"

"Well, it's unlikely the person who killed Sheila Broome would go *in* the cafe, isn't it? But assume he did. This waitress, you said, or Macalvie said, was very observant. Spotting the lorry, the driver, the girl in the rain." He shrugged. "It just seems odd she'd be so vague on the matter of identifying the picture, assuming, of course, there was something to identify. Perhaps, then, to her, it's a bit of a blur. . . . I was going back to Northants tomorrow. But I think I might just go to Exeter, if that's all right."

"Of course it's all right. But why?"

Melrose shook his head. "I don't know. Just a thought. Do you suppose I could have copies of these to take along?" He held up the photos.

"Sure. I'll have them made when I get to the Yard tonight and see you get copies in the morning." Jury turned. "Oh, hullo, William."

William Warboys was standing at his elbow, looking intent. As though the sudden appearance of his master signaled an ambush, Osmond made a dive for Melrose's foot.

Melrose winced. "Good Lord, can't you keep this hound on a lead?" He moved his foot in an arc, trying to dislodge Osmond.

Ignoring this, William said, "I worked out who killed Weldon."

"Weldon? Who killed Osmond would make a more satisfactory mystery."

"It was Sidney."

"Sidney? Sidney? I thought Sidney was Weldon's best friend."

"Well, he must not be, or he wouldn't have killed him," said William, reasonably. He then turned to Jury. "Want to go out back?"

"And what's out back?" asked Jury.

"Graves. It's a kind of cemetery. When something dies around here, I bury it." William looked down at his notebook. "It's where I get my inspiration."

Said Melrose, "It's where all of you get your inspiration."

17

MACALVIE sat with his feet on Jury's desk, his arms straitjacketed across his chest. His eyes shifted from watching Wiggins doctor his tea to the screen of a tiny portable television set, where an Oriental was detailing the joys of acupuncture. Wiggins kept the set in a filing cabinet and brought it out at noon every day for the acupuncture report.

"You'd think *someone* would've seen or heard something," said Wiggins, depositing two seltzer tablets into his mug and watching the bubbles sprout over its puce-colored surface.

"Someone did." Macalvie frowned. "What the hell's that, Wiggins? It looks like something's erupting in there." His hand went out for the folder that Jury had just discarded on his desk.

"This headache's fierce; it could turn migraine on me." Wiggins sipped his tea.

Macalvie grunted. "You make it sound like a rabid dog. There are two dozen houses in Hays Mews. Someone's not talking."

"Did you get hold of Andrew Starr, Wiggins?"

"Yes, sir. Said we'd go round to his place late this afternoon."

Macalvie's hat was down but the blue eyes glowed under the brim. "You'd think twice about having me go to Covent Garden, I figure."

Jury's smile was blinding. "Not twice. Once. You're welcome to talk to him once I've finished."

"Thanks. What about this friend of Marr's? Paul Swann?"

"Haven't talked to him yet. He's in Brighton."

Wiggins shivered. "At this time of year." He shook his head slowly.

"You can take off your coat, Macalvie. You won't be contaminated by the local police."

Macalvie undid two buttons. His eye wandered back to the TV, where the squirrel-like gibbering of the Oriental had been replaced by the news at twelve-twenty. Another terrorist attack at the Rome airport; a child drowned in the River Dart; an old man mugged. "Maybe there are things worse than murder," he said.

"Maybe, but I doubt it."

"Dante says—"

Jury looked up, startled. "Dante? You read Dante?" Jury opened another folder from the stack. "I never thought you had time to sit down and read a book."

"I wasn't sitting. An old guy was beaten up in his library. I was going through the books. He—Dante, I mean—puts it below murder: 'Betrayal of friends and benefactors.' Below murder, Jury." Macalvie took his feet from the desk, held out his hand for a Fisherman's Friend.

Wiggins was ripping open a package. "Getting a cold, sir?"

"No. I stopped smoking."

"Good. How long?"

Macalvie checked his watch. "Half-hour ago." He picked up a discarded folder. "What about this one? Says he was letting himself into his flat between eleven-thirty and midnight at that end of Charles Street."

"The pub closed at eleven."

"Yeah, but that doesn't mean she was killed at eleven."

"She wouldn't have been hanging round in Hays Mews for an hour."

Macalvie shrugged and tossed the folder on the desk. "No one can fix the time of death that closely. Although your pathologist didn't appreciate my telling her—"

Jury rubbed his fingers through his hair, leaving it standing up in licks. He sighed. "Macalvie, stop prowling the corridors, will you? Leave forensics alone."

Macalvie changed the subject. "This guy David Marr doesn't have any kind of an alibi. The servants were gone, the machine could have picked up the call. The sister's lying."

"Occasionally someone tells the truth, Macalvie."

Macalvie didn't look convinced. He ran his thumb down the stack of folders. "Someone knows something." He rewrapped his arms across his chest.

"What about Sheila Broome? Does someone know something there?"

"Of course."

Jury looked at him. "Nothing's turned up in ten months."

"Something will."

Jury picked up the telephone. "Jury here." The call was from Constable Whicker, on duty in the lobby.

"There's a lad down here, says his name is Colin Rees, says he may have something about the alleged murder in Hays Mews, sir."

Jury could have told it was Whicker from the way he qualified everything. Where Constable Whicker was concerned, "fact" was a relative term, and he always relayed information with caution signs pointing to it as if Fleet Street might be listening.

"Have someone bring him up, Constable."

Constable Whicker turned away from the telephone and there was a murmured exchange. "He appears not to want to, sir."

"Okay. I'll come down." He hung up and said to Macalvie, "There's a kid down in the lobby about the Hays Mews murder."

Macalvie shoved back his hat and smiled.

Two lads. The older of them, Colin Rees, eleven or twelve with faded blond hair the color of Horlicks and eyes like pebbles, small and gray. He carried a cap in his hands that looked several sizes too big for him, which he kept mashing together and pulling apart as if it were an accordion. He had the thin, tense look of a child used to being pinched in the playground.

"You're Colin Rees?"

"Colly, yes, sir." The boy shook Jury's outstretched hand. He was thin, with legs like spindles and fingers like dry twigs.

"I'm Superintendent Jury. This is Divisional Commander Macalvie." The boy nodded at Macalvie with the solemnity of an acolyte. "This here's my brother, Jimmy. Say hello, Jimmy."

That Jimmy, who was a stubbier version of Colly, wasn't going to say "hello" was made clear by the head turned to the floor as if the eyes meant to drill a hole through the divisional commander's shoes.

Colly Rees shrugged. "Jimmy never did talk much before Uncle Bub got after him about that lady and now he don't talk at all. Uncle Bub said we was to stay straight out of it. Well, he's not a proper uncle, he ain't, but—"

"Let's sit down, Colly. Jimmy?"

Jimmy stood like a stump, his eyes on Macalvie's shoes.

Colly, sitting half-on, half-off one of the leather benches that lined the lobby wall, said to Jury, pumping up his lungs for another go, "What happened was, Jimmy and me was inside the pub—"

"What were you and Jimmy doing *inside?*" asked Wiggins, looking a little fretful at the possibility of a violation of the licensing laws.

"Oh, well, we was just waiting in the kitchen. For Uncle Bub. He kind of caretakes the place and he was closing up. Me and Jimmy'd come from the fillums down in Curzon Street."

Jury looked up at Macalvie, whose silence was being bought at the price of a stare that could have nailed Colly Rees to the wall. "Go on, then," he said to Colly.

"It was Jimmy saw her. He was standing on a bench, looking out through the window at the rain."

"Saw who?"

"This lady, sir. Well, that's what Jimmy says. Now me, I was near the side door that was still open. And I heard someone running. It must have been the same lady, sir." He was crushing his hat up into a ball in his earnestness.

"You heard her. You didn't see her?"

Colly Rees shook his head impatiently and twisted his cap. "It was Jimmy done the seeing. Well, see, we neither of us dihn't think nothing of it, just somebody running in the rain. It was only after we was watching the telly and heard the news about that lady getting—" Colly jerked his scarf about his neck. Wiggins winced.

"Okay. Go on, Colly."

"Nothing to be going on with, except it was a lady."

"Jimmy?" said Jury to the little one's back. Jimmy Rees hadn't moved an inch since he'd taken up his station by Macalvie's shoes. And Macalvie, thought Jury, was making the supreme sacrifice: he hadn't cuffed, slugged, or shouted at him.

Colly said: "Oh, you won't get nothing outta Jimmy, sir. Acts like he's deaf as a post when he wants to."

"Didn't he describe this lady?"

"No. 'The rainlady' he calls her." He looked at his brother, whose head bobbed slightly like an apple on a branch, perhaps by way of confirmation.

Jury looked at Macalvie and back at Colly. "It was raining. Is that what he means?"

"I don't know, sir, do I? Whenever I ask him all he says is, ' 'T was the rainlady.' He frowned at Jimmy's back, as if this runic message better not pop out inside the walls of New Scotland Yard. "And Aunt Nettie she talked to him something fierce about telling stories, and give him a box round the ears, and give Uncle Bub one, too, for letting us stop in that pub. Said she'd do us both proper if we was to say anything about that night."

"I wouldn't worry about Aunt Nettie, Colly—"

"I don't guess you would. She ain't your aunt, is she? But she says she won't let us watch the telly or have no sweets. Jimmy just loves the telly, that's why he don't talk much. He'd as soon let everybody else do it. I asked him and asked him, dihn't I? And that's all he says. ' 'Twas the rainlady.' "

Macalvie pried his eyes from the downturned head of Jimmy Rees and beamed them on his older brother. "You said you heard running footsteps. How'd you know it was a woman?"

"Well, I guess it had to be, dihn't it, if Jimmy here *saw* a lady?" he said reasonably.

"That's not what I asked: I asked what you *heard*."

"She was running, sir. I mean, '*it*,' " he added as a quick qualification. " 'It' was running, sir."

Macalvie bestowed upon Colly a smile like splintered wood. "I mean, how could you tell she or he was running?"

With his tongue he made a clicking sound against the roof of his mouth: "It was them high heels. I never did know a man to wear them."

"Running?"

"Yes, sir."

"Walking fast, maybe."

"Running."

"Walking."

Wiggins looked from Macalvie to first one boy and then the other. "Sir, does it make that much difference?"

Macalvie glared. "You decide if it's the truth first. You decide if it makes a difference second." He turned back to Colly. "Let's say it was a woman," he graciously allowed. "You wouldn't have heard the tap of the heels; the heels wouldn't have hit the ground if she'd been running. So she was walking fast."

"Either way, she might have seen something, Macalvie." Jury turned to Colly. "Okay, Colly, it was certainly brave of you to come here. Both you and Jimmy."

Jimmy did not respond to pronouncements on heroism. He kept his eyes on the shoes.

"Sergeant Wiggins here can take you home. Where do you live?"

"Near Wapping Old Stairs, sir."

Macalvie was tearing open another pack of gum. "I can do it," he said. "You?"

"Sure. Maybe get some sweets, some ice cream along the way. What do you say, kids?"

Colly said Jimmy liked chocolate flake; Jimmy did not confirm this.

Jury smiled and shook his head. There were moments when kids were just not going to open up—maybe later, but not now, chewing gum and chocolate flake notwithstanding. "Decent of you, Macalvie."

"No problem. Maybe we can have a little talk about this lady."

As if the voice were coming out of the floor and transmitted by the divisional commander's shoes, Jimmy said, " 'Twas the rainlady."

PART IV

Stardust Melody

18

〜✦〜

THE house in Knightsbridge faced one of those small green parks surrounded by a wrought-iron fence whose gate could only be unlocked with a key. There was no one else up and down the street and no traffic. Jury often marveled at the silence of such neighborhoods; even traffic kept its distance. Several blocks away cars and buses moved along Sloane Street. Jury looked at the cars parked in front of the house: a white Lotus Elan, dropped, really, like a blossom between the long, black Jaguar and the sable brown Mercedes. As he waited, an elderly woman with two Labradors unlatched the gate of the park and went in.

He looked above the door, at the stained glass and the pediment into which had been carved a coat of arms, now faded. The woman who opened the door, probably a housekeeper, was short and curt. If she was surprised at seeing Jury's warrant card, she hid it well.

Hugh Winslow was a tall, spare man somewhere in his middle sixties who probably kept in shape by regular exercise on tennis and squash courts. His eyes were very blue in the sunlamp-tan of his face, the skin tight over the cheekbones, the complexion like parchment. The body relaxed when he settled into the deep armchair in which he had been, apparently, reading; his manner was that of a man who had solved all of his problems some time back, and he looked at Jury as if whatever had brought police to his door was either inconsequential or a mistake altogether.

"What can I do for you, Superintendent? Would you care for a drink?" He started to get up.

"No, thanks. I'd just like to ask you a few questions, Mr. Winslow, having to do with a young lady who was murdered four nights ago near a pub called I Am the Only Running Footman. Do you know it?"

"No, I don't think I do."

"Your brother-in-law frequented it."

"I've visited David a few times in Shepherd Market, but I've not been to that pub—" He broke off.

"I didn't say Shepherd Market."

Winslow fumbled for both cigarettes and words. "I was simply assuming—"

"I see. Perhaps you've talked with your wife or your brother-in-law?"

"Yes, that's it."

You should have thought of that before I did, thought Jury. "David Marr was, so far as anyone knows, the last person to see Ivy Childess alive. He's in a spot. I wondered if you could tell me anything about him."

"David and I see very little of one another, Superintendent. He comes here infrequently, usually when Ned is here."

"Your son."

"Yes."

"And are you on good terms with him?"

Hugh Winslow's answer was oblique. "He used to stay here when he came to London. Now he's taken rooms in Belgravia."

"But how do you get on?"

"Not very well. He's excessively fond of his mother, though. They both are, Ned and David." His smile was strained.

"What do you mean, 'excessively'?"

Hugh Winslow stubbed out the cigarette and poured himself a whiskey. "I simply meant 'extremely,' that's all. It's not unnatural, especially where Marion is concerned. She's the sort of woman who calls up strong feelings in men."

"In you, Mr. Winslow?"

He looked at Jury over the rim of his glass. "I don't see what this has to do with—Miss Childess."

Jury smiled. "Humor me."

Winslow sighed. "Marion and I are somewhat—estranged. We have been ever since our daughter died."

"I'm sorry about your daughter, Mr. Winslow."

"Yes." He got up and started to wander about the room aimlessly, poking up the fire, moving to the high window. Jury was reminded of Marion Winslow. "It happened just out there," he said, nodding toward the street. "The man responsible wasn't sentenced—it wasn't, I suppose, his fault. He seemed, actually, a decent chap. Wells, or something, was his name."

"Miles Wells. I've checked the accident report. Ten o'clock at night, wasn't it?"

Abstractedly, Hugh nodded, continued his own train of thought. "Yes, I suppose so. It's difficult being thought perfect, you know; that's the way they seemed to think about Phoebe. It must have left her very little room to breathe. Like other children, she had a temper. She was only a little girl, not a holy icon. But everything seemed to change, with that."

"Until her death, you and your wife were quite happy, were you?"

"I'd say so, yes."

"Yet, there were other women, Mr. Winslow."

Hugh Winslow had returned to his chair by the fire. It was a dark leather wing chair, and again Jury was reminded of that meeting with his wife. An odd feeling, like déjà vu.

Hugh's smile was a little chilly. "Well, that's true. You might not understand it, but Marion is about the most perfect woman I've ever known—"

"And it was difficult for you to live with perfection."

He nodded. "But if it's David you've come about, you'd be better off asking Marion." He started to pour himself another drink.

Hugh Winslow seemed as isolated as the privileged strollers in the park across the street; it would need a key to get in.

"I have talked with her; it isn't David Marr I wanted to ask you about, particularly. It's Ivy Childess."

The decanter froze in midair. Then he put it down, replaced the stopper, and said, "I really don't know what you mean." It was a poor effort to regain his composure. The key had turned; the gate was open.

"I mean that you knew Ivy Childess."

"I met her once. It was here, at a small cocktail party."

"And you'd met her since, hadn't you? At the Running Footman."

He looked over at the dying fire. Then he turned and said, "Yes."

"But why see her at the pub your brother-in-law often went to?" Jury thought he knew the answer to that.

And it was confirmed when Winslow said it had been Ivy's idea; she liked the place. "But they knew nothing about Ivy and me. Marion certainly didn't."

"Are you sure she didn't suspect?"

"Yes. If she had—"

"If she had, she might have divorced you, is that it?"

"Ivy kept up her relationship with David simply so no one would suspect."

Perhaps he really believed that. "Was she holding out for marriage? Did she threaten to make a scene?" Jury knew he was right from the unhappy look Hugh Winslow gave him. "Which is perhaps a price you weren't prepared to pay. Your wife has a great deal of money in her own right."

"I am not exactly a pauper, Superintendent. Oh, you're right, in a way. I wasn't prepared to pay the price. I love Marion; I had no intention of marrying Ivy."

Jury was silent for a moment. His mind had turned to the talk with Stella Broome. *Flash cars and flash men.* Like Ivy Childess, in a way. "Mr. Winslow, about ten months ago there was a young woman murdered in a wood off the road between Exeter and Bristol. Her name was Sheila Broome. Mean anything to you?"

Hugh Winslow seemed relieved that they had left the subject of Ivy Childess. "No, no, I've never heard the name."

"The end of February. The twenty-ninth, it was."

He tried to laugh, but it caught in his throat. "Superintendent, you seem to be asking me where I was."

Jury smiled. "That's right."

Winslow's voice frosted over. "I believe I was out of the country. I have offices in Paris. But I can certainly check my calendar, although I doubt that particular appointment would be noted, were I going to Devon."

"Check it anyway, Mr. Winslow. Is that your Jaguar outside?"

He seemed confused. "Well, no. The Mercedes is mine. Why?"

"Ever own a Jaguar?"

"Of course." He shrugged.

Hasn't everyone? Jury smiled. "When was that?"

"Oh, two or three years ago, I expect. But I don't see why—?"

"You said you had no intention of marrying Ivy. That sounds very much like what your brother-in-law said."

Winslow shifted uncomfortably in his chair. "Ivy was—well, she was a terrible opportunist. And I've never known anyone so adept at finding out things. The sort of woman you confide in and wish you hadn't—" He stopped.

Jury thought for a moment. "Would your brother-in-law be likely to confide in her?"

"David? Probably; he's a much softer person than people suppose. But I'm not sure what there would have been to confide; David is very open."

Given that Hugh had been excluded from the family circle, Jury thought him to be fairly charitable. "Mr. Marr seems to have run through a great deal of money, your wife said. And he seems fond of going off to places like Cannes and Monte Carlo—" An image of David Marr's pleasantly sloppy bulletin board came to Jury's mind. "Has he ever been to America?"

Hugh Winslow frowned. "Not that I know of. None of us has. Rose— that was Edward's wife—used to talk about going there. I've always wanted—"

"Yes, so've I. David Marr does not really seem to have expensive tastes, although he talks about gambling, casinos, the fast life. It makes me wonder about the money he's run through."

"I can't imagine David buying Ivy's silence. David's much more the publish-and-be-damned type."

"Depends on what might get published, I expect. And what about you, Mr. Winslow? Are you the same type?"

Startled, Winslow turned away. "I imagine I did let Ivy borrow a bit."

"Borrow. How much would a 'bit' be?"

"A few thousand." Hastily, he added, as if it would justify the loan, "She wanted to buy into the shop she worked in as assistant. It's in Covent Garden—"

"Perhaps that's your idea of 'small'; it's not mine. A blackmailer might call it 'small,' of course."

Winslow looked ashen.

"That accident to your little girl happened around ten—"

"What does *that* have to do with it?"

"Perhaps a great deal. At ten o'clock at night, Phoebe ran out into the street. You say she had tantrums. Is that by way of explaining why an eight-year-old would run out into a dark street late at night? Or was there some other reason? Although Edward was here, you say, he wasn't staying here. That meant you were here with Phoebe. And someone else, possibly."

"Ivy was here," he said, his head propped up by his hand, like something broken. "Phoebe saw us." He looked upward, as if visualizing a scene on the floor above. "It was dreadful." His head dropped in his hand again. "But she wasn't blackmailing me, Superintendent."

"Not technically, perhaps. But didn't it come to the same thing? 'A few thousand quid, and I won't tell Marion what happened that night'?"

Winslow didn't answer.

Jury rose and said, "I'll want to talk with you later."

Hugh Winslow saw him to the door, where he said, as if they were still speaking about her, "The price would have been Marion. I'm already a pariah, I expect. They don't communicate much anymore." He looked very weary.

"Yes," was all of Jury's answer. A pariah. Standing in the hall, Jury looked at him with sympathy, thought of his isolation. They had sent him to Coventry.

He looked back from the pavement to see the man still framed in the doorway, the pediment with its faded coat of arms above him, origins probably long forgotten.

In the little park across the way one or two people walked, enjoying privacy and privilege.

19

THERE once was a marketplace, but it had been replaced by a grimly commercial double-storied shopping mall with its collection of boutiques, forbidding health food restaurants, candy shops, card shops, novelty shops, all of them charging inflated prices because of the address. Jury preferred cabbages and fishmongers. So did Wiggins, apparently.

"I liked it the other way; I liked them selling fresh vegetables and so forth. I wish the Council would just have left it alone, so what if it was a bit grotty and smelly. That was London, after all."

"You're right, Wiggins. That was London."

Blue neon shading into silver stuttered out the shop's name, Starrdust. Against the black background, the last three letters trailed off into another dimension, dusted with silver.

The shop faced Covent Garden's new marketplace—at least Jury would always think of it as new. As he stood with Wiggins and looked into the window, Jury thought Starrdust might even be a sort of oasis amidst all of this clamor, the rush of rock music rolling in waves from shop fronts; the endless trade in records and jeans and croissant sandwiches.

At first Jury thought it must be a magic shop. Against a cloth backdrop of black velvet (itself sprinkled with silver dust) the window displayed black-coned hats with gold quarter moons, ebony wands topped with fake jeweled stars, silver cutouts of planets hanging by invisible threads. And off to one side was a little house in the woods, and out of this house on an electrified rail came a mechanical Merlin, in his black and starry cape and hat, clutching a tiny wand that he raised once as if in benediction before he rolled silently home.

"Did you see that, sir?" said Wiggins, apparently unaware of the three children that had lately gathered for the wizard performance.

Jury studied the cardboard constellations, names dangling on bits of silver string—Pluto, Scorpio—down through all of the signs of the zodiac. And a sun, giving off a pale wintry light that directed one's attention to a large book, opened, with illuminated writing. And farther down a small gold sign said "Horoscopes and Rare Books." The shop catered not for magicians but for fatalists.

When Jury cupped his hands and looked through the glass of the door (that also bore a sign "Shop assistant wanted"), he thought the place must be closed for lunch, it was so dark. Yet Wiggins had called to say they were coming. He turned the knob and the door opened. Wiggins dragged himself away from Merlin and the three children and followed him.

Like a theater that takes a little getting used to, Starrdust was appropriately cave-dark. Jury blinked. The room was quite long and narrow, and he could not see into its farthest reaches. Whoever had done the place up was highly imaginative. If it was Andrew Starr, he had had the good fortune of never quite growing up. There were lights in the place, bright points of light, that made Jury remember reading under the covers with a flashlight. The room got vaguely lighter. Off in one corner was a child-sized house, painted in the neon blue of the sign, covered with astrological symbols and with a bright sign over its door: *Horror-Scopes.* The three children who didn't look like they'd a pence between them had swarmed in with Jury and Wiggins and made for the playhouse. They were obviously well acquainted with the wonders of Starrdust. Against the long wall several tall bookcases were spaced. Between them on the wall hung silver-framed photos of film stars, long-ago ones like Judy Garland, Ronald Colman. They all looked out of the past amid a spattering of stars and little moons. Jury looked at the books and saw they were indeed antiquarian stuff, stacked among the moons and stars like a lunar library.

The pièce de résistance had already been discovered by Wiggins, who was gazing up at a domed ceiling of which the owner had taken best advantage and made into a sort of mock planetarium. "Look at that," said Wiggins again. "Like Madame Tussaud's that one is."

"Not quite," said Jury, star-gazing up himself. "See, there goes Venus—" A light dimmed behind the planet. "—and here comes Mars." A light switched silently on. The star-works continued operating its little lights and giving the eerie feeling that the skies were moving.

"Feel like I'm floating," said Wiggins.

From the horror-house came an almost drowsy laughter.

From somewhere in the rear came the Tin-Panny sound of Hoagy Carmichael's "Stardust." But there was no blare, no stereo. Surprisingly the record, which sounded very scratched, was being played on a simple record player. Time seemed to stretch like the room itself. Jury actually checked his watch, although he knew they'd only been here a minute or less.

Out of the well at the rear, two girls of probably nineteen or twenty came forward. They were dressed in gray cords and black peasant blouses with some sort of silvery thread that winked in the light of the planetarium-ceiling. They both had pale hair held back with star-crusted combs; pale, almost opalescent skin; eyes shaded in blue and silver, pearly-pink lipstick so that the light that washed over them turned to a dissolving rainbow. One might have thought they were twins, though they weren't; weren't, perhaps, even sisters. One asked if they could help. The other giggled slightly. The first gave her a look of warning. Yet they exuded such an air of good humor, Jury couldn't help but laugh himself a little, seeing them standing there straight, each with an arm round the other's waist, like skaters on a pond.

At Jury's response, their clear faces grew even brighter, if that were possible, almost as if the lights behind the planets had switched on behind their eyes. He showed them his warrant card.

"Oh!" said one of the stardust twins. "It's Andrew you'll be wanting to see. See, he told us to look out for two coppers—" She coughed and blushed and said, sorry, "—but you neither of you look nothing like police. . . ."

Jury smiled as her voice trailed off. Wiggins probably didn't look like much of anything except a star-gazer. He was still at it. "Andrew Starr, is it? My sergeant talked to him earlier."

"Andrew, that's right. We'll just get him." The stardust twins apparently did everything in two's. There were fresh giggles, but not from the girls. "It's them kids again, Meg," said one. "Oh, Andy don't mind," said the other. Mind or not, they shooed the children out of the painted house. They trooped about for a bit, looking but not touching, and then came to stand and stare, openmouthed, gap-toothed, up at Jury, who knew not what precisely they were assessing him for, but to take no chances, he plunked down a ten-p piece and took three jelly babies from the glass bowl.

They looked at one another, smiled a little, and then trooped out. Another day in the Starrdust.

Andrew Starr had come in on their exiting coattails and looked at them now on the outside staring in at the toy Merlin. He shook his head. "They're here several times a week," he said without introduction. "A few of the regulars. Like a pub, the Starrdust is. It's got its regulars."

Jury looked at Wiggins, still transfixed by the stars, and thought the Starrdust might have added one more to its list.

Andrew Starr was a good-looking young man, slight but well built and well dressed, a person who could make his unexceptionable outfit—tailored cotton shirt and jeans—look as if they came from a bespoke tailor. His hair and eyes were dark, his bones finely structured. He wore a heavy pendant, probably his own astrological sign, and a gold link bracelet, which he habitually turned.

"Of course, it's about Ivy, isn't it?" Starr sat down behind his counter and fished a cigarette from a porcelain mug. He lit up and offered the cigarettes to Jury. Wiggins had finally come down to earth and was getting out his notebook. The stardust twins were shelving books from a crate.

"Ivy Childess, yes. How long had she been working here?"

"Year or less. Had a job behind a counter at Boots before she came here. Ivy was much too ambitious to spend her days dusting eyeshadow on middle-aged women."

"Ambitious?"

"Oh, my, yes. There were three words to describe Ivy. Ambition, ambition, ambition. Of course, she was very good here—"

"What'd she do, exactly?"

"Shop assistant; as you see, I'm looking for another one. Sorry, that sounds a bit macabre. Well, I just can't get all worked up about Ivy. I didn't honestly like her much, but as I said, she was damned good. Besides that"—Starr reached beneath the counter—"she was a pretty good Madame Zostra."

He had brought out a spangled satin wraparound headpiece, something like a turban, and a large pack of cards, the tarot deck. Jury smiled. "Ivy told fortunes, did she?"

Andrew Starr smiled broadly. "For fun, for entertainment. No attempt to rip off the clientele. Much as she wanted to," he added dryly.

Jury spread out the cards. "You don't believe in all this, then?"

Starr looked a little wounded. "Of course I do. Astrology, that is. And most of my customers I've had for ages." He looked toward the photographs between the bookcases. "Theater, film stars. Well, not them up there. Guess they're all dead. Never did see Marilyn Monroe, worse luck."

Jury smiled. "You'd have been much too young to appreciate her."

"Not for Marilyn Monroe."

"Did Ivy believe in the tarot, astrology, that sort of thing?"

"Oh, good heavens, no. That's probably why she was better at selling stuff. She could sell a pig a silver trough. No, but she knew a good thing— Starrdust *is* a good thing, I can tell you—"

"I believe it, Mr. Starr."

"Andrew. Call me Andrew. Well, Ivy had a bit of money and she kept nagging me to buy in. Wanted to be my partner, she did. I didn't pay any attention to her because I thought she hadn't any more than a few hundred quid—what I mean is, I didn't really bother saying I didn't *want* a partner. Well, she must have taken this as encouragement. Comes in one day with a check for two thousand quid. Then, of course, I put her right off. Said I didn't need a partner. But the damned girl—sorry—Ivy was as tenacious as her name. If she wanted something, she just *went* for it. Power was what she wanted, and money meant power. Take this chap, David, she went about with—"

"David Marr."

"Poor devil. He came in here a few times before closing, hung about, waiting for her. I thought he was a pleasant fellow myself. You know, it's odd the way some people, no matter how simply they dress and talk, simply *reek* of money. Marr was one. So of course she hung on to him. Pardon." He reached behind him and spun another record onto the machine. It was scratchy, like the first. The voice of Dinah Shore singing "Stars Fell on Alabama."

"Ivy wanted to marry him, you think?"

Andrew hooted. "My God, but didn't she. The man was *loaded*. Well, would have been. She talked a lot about what he'd come into. As if she were coming into it too, of course. Only, you know, he didn't seem all that interested. At least not in marrying Ivy. But I suppose she thought she'd wear down his resistance; she'd sit here and flip through the cards and keep saying she'd an 'ace' up her sleeve."

"What do you think she meant by that?"

He shrugged. "Dunno." Andrew twisted the gold bracelet round and round his wrist and frowned. "You know, I think this Marr fellow thought at first he was getting a sweet little shop-girl in Ivy, and then found out she was a grasping, cold-hearted little bitch. Sorry."

"No need to apologize, Andrew. The dead are no more likable because they're dead."

Andrew Starr relaxed and lit another cigarette. "If you want to know what *I* think, it's that her boyfriend really did want to settle down. Probably, in a little cottage in Kent or somewhere—"

Jury smiled. "That's not exactly my impression of David Marr."

"I'm extremely intuitive, Superintendent. Seriously." He looked round the room. "I've always been fascinated with this sort of thing—when was Marr born, do you know?"

Jury calculated. "Nineteen forty-six. I'd have to check the month and day."

"And hour. Find out that for me and I can tell just what kind of person he is."

Jury had heard of using clairvoyants to solve crimes, but not astrologers. "Thanks. We can use all the help we can get. But do you think he was capable of murder?"

To Jury's surprise, Andrew Starr did not immediately say no. Instead, he gazed up at his mock-planetarium, and finally said, "Oh, he seems very cool, but he's the sort who might do anything—murder, even—if he's terribly disillusioned."

Wiggins looked up from his notebook. "That 'ace' up her sleeve, sir. Would you say she might have known something about David Marr?"

"Possible. In some way she certainly thought she could trump Marr's trick—No. No. No, children—"

This was addressed to the stardust twins, who were in the process of hanging the mirror that had been resting against the bookshelves. One of them stood on a short ladder, the other was holding the mirror at the bottom.

"—a little bit higher. That's right."

It was an odd sort of mirror, a combination of mirror and kaleidoscope. From its fractured center, chips of color turned and reflected in spangles on the twins' faces. "Where'd you get that?" asked Jury.

"Antiques shop in Brighton. I thought it would fit here. The kaleidoscope effect is an optical illusion."

"Brighton?"

Andrew nodded. "Used to live in Hove. I did a fair business in Brighton with horoscopes. You know it's quite famous for looking into the future— if one can put it that way. The place has got a long tradition of astrologers and clairvoyants and so forth. Of course, it's a seaside town, so perhaps that's to be expected. Most of them are honest, I'd say. One or two quite brilliant. I was never one of the one or two," he said ruefully. "Still, I'm honest."

Wiggins was watching the mirror-event with great fascination. "Don't you think, sir, I should just go and give the young ladies a hand?" Without waiting for Jury to agree, he put his notebook on the counter and went off.

"Interesting. We've got to talk to someone in Brighton." Since it was Wiggins whom Jury was going to have do the talking to, he was glad he was out of earshot; Wiggins didn't much fancy seaside resorts, winter or summer. Winter, especially, spelled certain death. "Did you ever know Ivy Childess to go there?"

"Not to my knowledge. As I said, Ivy didn't believe in much of anything but cold, hard cash. Your sergeant seems to be right at home—" He nodded toward the mirror-event. "—if he ever tires of the Met, think he'd like a job?"

Jury smiled. "That's the sign in the window, is it? Speaking of that, have you had any response?"

"Oh, yes. Quite a bit. But they don't really suit, somehow." Andrew shrugged. They're either condescending or crass." He looked up at the planets. "They seem to think it's all a joke, or cleverly commercial, or unworthy of their considerable talents."

"The reason I ask is I have a friend who just might do you. Well, if you can take someone a little bit zany. But hardworking and loyal and very, very pretty."

"Sounds divine. As to the zany, good; that's our style. And as to the *pretty,* all the better. Customers like it, and so do I. A pretty face lifts the spirits, Superintendent, wouldn't you say?"

"I certainly would." He looked at the stardust twins, who with Wiggins's help had hung the glass from the neon heavens. The three of them were standing, looking up at it, making fun-house faces, splattered with rainbow-chips. "Are they sisters?"

"Meg and Joy? Oh, no. A lot of people think they're twins, even. I have them dress alike and I suppose again it's a kind of illusion. Most people see what they want to, or at least what they expect to. No, Meg and Joy came in one day when I needed a clerk. They just stood there, looking beamish, and their poor faces fell when I told them I only needed the one. They looked *so* unhappy that I just hired them both. I couldn't bear separating them, I hated to break up the set." He smiled. "But I haven't been sorry. Do you know, they've been here for nearly two years, and in all that time I haven't heard one cross word between them. Plenty of cross words from Ivy, though. And she couldn't stand Meg and Joy. To me that says a lot about Ivy Childess. Not only was I not going to make her a partner, I was going to fire her."

"That bad, was she?"

"That bad. To tell the truth, I'm surprised it wasn't the other way round, her being killed. I mean I'd say she'd have been more liable to kill Marr for refusing to marry her. Poor bloke."

"Did she ever mention any other men, Andrew? Could that have been the ace up her sleeve?"

Andrew Starr thought for a moment. "I honestly can't remember any other man ever being mentioned. He'd have to be rich."

"Or someone who might very well have made David Marr jealous."

"Him jealous? Oh, no, I don't think so. In fact I think Marr and I had the same thing in mind: dump her."

"She wouldn't have taken kindly to dumping." Jury pocketed Wiggins's notebook and got up. "Andrew, I appreciate your help."

"Happy to. And tell that friend of yours to call and set up a time we can get together. Or she can just come round, but the place tends to get very busy." Andrew wrote on the back of a Starrdust card and handed the card to Jury. "There's another number here. Ex-directory. The business line can get terribly tied up. We're closed today, actually. We left the door open for you and your sergeant."

"Well, I'll just collect my sergeant and be on my way." He called to Wiggins, who turned unhappily from the mirror and came back to the counter, in a wake of giggles. The stardust twins went about polishing the mirror.

"I like your shop, Mr. Starr. Bet the kiddies find it a sort of paradise, with all the lights and stars and that little house over there." Wiggins nodded toward *Horror-Scopes.*

"They do, yes. Not been inside that, Sergeant?" Andrew slid a bit of a smile in Jury's direction as Wiggins hesitated, looking at the house.

"Don't tempt him. Thanks again."

"That's all right. I hardly feel I've been questioned by police." He smiled.

"There might be someone coming along to ask a few questions. The Devon police have an interest in this case. Anyway"—Jury smiled—"you might feel you've been questioned by police then."

"I'll be watching out for them. Good-bye, Superintendent. Sergeant." They shook hands as the stardust twins watched. The one on her ladder perch waved the dustcloth.

On the pavement, Jury blinked. "A nice fellow; a nice place."

"You know, sir, all of that fooling about with the mirror—I hope you didn't think I was larking."

"No, of course not. Anyway, we all need a bit of a lark now and then." They were walking toward the Covent Garden tube station.

"What I was really doing, was asking a few discreet questions of the girls."

"Oh? Did you find out anything, then?" Jury looked away, smiling.

Wiggins walked along deep in thought. To help it along, he drew out his tube of lozenges. "Only that they didn't really know anything, sir. But they did ask me round to their place for tea and a chat sometime. Here, do you need their address?"

"Just keep it handy, Wiggins. You never know. Here's the station." They looked up at the blue and red sign. "It's going to be pretty, isn't it, when they finally finish." He nodded toward the scaffolding outside. "Going to be done in a garden motif. Well, it's Covent Garden, isn't it?"

"True. We're not going to be seeing too much of gardens in the next few days. I want to talk to Marr's friend, Paul Swann, so I just thought we'd go down to Brighton in the morning."

The lozenges might have done for the London market; Brighton, however, hard by the sea, necessitated the drawing out of Wiggins's handkerchief. "Brighton, sir." He blew his nose and, without even as yet casting his eye on the cold sea, or lifting his face to the cold sea air, he looked as if he were coming down with sea-virus. "That's right by the sea, sir."

"I know." It occurred to Jury that not once in the Starrdust had Wiggins gone for nose drops, handkerchief, lozenges. Jury stared up at a sky as unyielding as cement. "Hard falling back to earth, isn't it?"

20

⚓️

KATE looked up at the high, huge dome, the silver-winged dragon, the star of mirror glass, the open flowers, and the ropes of jewels from which hung the splendid chandelier and wondered what it must have been like when the room was alight. An artificial day created by a blaze of diamonds.

On the other side of the red velvet cord, Kate was the only visitor now. The half-dozen others who had been wandering about were no longer to be seen. The guard at the end of the banqueting table looked bored, impatient to be home, probably; he had ceased long ago to be impressed by gilded serpents and silver dragons and jewels. Perhaps he thought of it as some sort of joke, some hoax, the sort of thing that royalty was always getting up to. He yawned and clasped his hands behind his back.

Her mind, she supposed, was no less mundane, no less homeward-looking. In the midst of this splendor—what exotic dishes must have been served up at that table!—she thought of the meal she must fix, the carrots and cabbage left out. Carrots and cabbage.

Kate dug her hands into her coat pockets, her purse trolling from her wrist, and wondered what Dolly was doing, where she was. They had had another of their arguments about the bed-and-breakfast business, letting the room to a stranger. I beg your pardon, Dolly, but that's generally the sort who books rooms: strangers. Who was he? What did she know about him? Didn't she realize it could be dangerous?

He had hardly looked dangerous. He looked, indeed, quite attractive, quite interesting. Had she told Dolly she had met him in the Spotted Dog —well, all hell would have broken loose. Kate sighed. To meet someone in a pub and offer him a room, knowing nothing about him . . .

A guard was at her elbow, telling her quietly that it was just on five, closing time. How long had she been standing here? As she walked out into the long corridor, the question remained: What did she know about him except that he was charming? Nothing. He came from London, and what did that mean? Perhaps Dolly was right this time. But then Dolly did not share her, Kate's, loneliness.

Under a ceiling divided by small trellises, Kate walked through the reds and blues, bamboo and porcelain, and wondered what sort of man, what sort of king, could build himself this fantasy world. Whose lives had he ruined, whose hearts had he wrecked in the fashioning?

Kate made her way across Castle Square. A light rain lifted and billowed like a delicate curtain and there were few other people in the square, which is why she noticed the man at the far end of the long walk. It was too far away to tell absolutely, but she thought he resembled the man she'd met in the Spotted Dog. He did not move; he seemed to be looking at her.

It made her nervous, although she knew it was ridiculous. He was observing the Royal Pavilion, not Kate. She stopped and turned and looked back. The exquisite architecture of the Pavilion's facade was sorely borne upon by high scaffolding. Most of the workmen had left, but two still sat up there, smoking and drinking from Styrofoam cups. A building full of silver dragons and diamonds and dry rot. She stuffed her hair up under her knitted cap and thought that the reality was the scaffolding, not the silver and gilt. The workmen flicked their cigarettes over the edge, took their belongings, quit, unaware they were patching up a fantasy. Buildings rot, that meant jobs.

When Kate turned again, the man was gone.

21

❦

THREE floors up, Carole-anne Palutski was reeling in the undies pinned to a rope she'd rigged between windowsill and close-hanging branch. The row of bright-colored bikini panties billowed slightly in the wind up there, like flags on a yacht. In the Islington house, there were just the three of them—Mrs. Wassermann in the basement flat, Jury on the ground floor, Carole-anne two floors above, where the rent was cheaper. The middle flat was vacant, and Carole-anne had convinced the landlord to let her "show" it. This was done not simply for the reduced rent it allowed her, but to make sure that if anyone got in, it would be someone who would not upset their clubby threesome.

"Hi, Super!" she called, waving her free hand hysterically as if she didn't see him every day. The undies shot in; the head disappeared.

Jury went up the steps to his Islington flat, first looking to see if Mrs. Wassermann was in. These days, with Carole-anne around, Mrs. Wassermann had become less fearful of the London streets, had taken to going out more to the shops and the butcher's and the greengrocer's.

As Jury went up, Carole-anne ran down, her espadrilles slap, slap, slapping on the staircase, her bottle of bright coral nail varnish in one hand. She had finished one set of fingers and one set of toes. They just missed a collision in front of his door, which didn't surprise Jury; she'd caused enough out in the street. Carole-anne was the only person he knew who could saunter across Piccadilly Circus nonstop. Today she was wearing blinding pink shorts and top that made a surprising blend with her red-gold hair. Only, some of that hair had been dyed an even deeper red since he'd seen her five days ago. Hot coral, brazen pink, brassy orange, fiery licks of hair.

"Hello, Carole-anne; you look like a Tijuana sunset." As they went into his flat, he asked her what she'd done to her hair.

"Now you'll be on about it, I expect," she said crossly, as she flopped herself on his sprung sofa and finished applying the polish to her other toes. Then, "Oh," she said carelessly, unfolding herself and pulling a piece of notepaper from the waistband of her shorts. "Here. It's from SB-stroke-H."

Carole-anne refused actually to *name* Susan Bredon-Hunt, as if by this magical incantation, the person named might appear out of fire and smoke on the spot. Jury looked at the note and its terse message: *eight o'clock.*

Now, Jury knew that Susan Bredon-Hunt was not a woman of few words. He waved the paper. "This all? No flowery tribute to New Scotland Yard and its minions, me being minion number one? No frills and furbelows? No, 'love, Susan'?" He sat down and pulled out his cigarettes and wondered if he had any more beer.

"You needn't get shirty," Carole-anne said, huffing it out. She was now half-reclining on the sofa, her legs raised in the air, the small of her back propped with her hands. "I'm only the bloody answering service, I am."

Jury smiled. Well, it was true. Carole-anne loved to come in and answer his telephone and play her records on his old record player. He sometimes came home and heard the keening wail of Tiny Rudy, her favorite vocalist, or the calamity-in-the-kitchen sounds (breaking crockery and crystal) of Ticket to Hell, her favorite rock group. Given this access to his flat, Carole-anne had decided three months ago that her favorite policeman should have it redecorated and (naturally without his knowledge) had called Decors, one of the swankiest outfits in London, to come round with their swatches.

Her largess with imaginary money was then forgotten, but the swatches had turned up all the same, in the hand of Susan Bredon-Hunt—tall, model-thin, high-fashion clothes, hair razor cut . . .

It was beginning to sound metallic. All Carole-anne's doing, with her various descriptions of Susan. Her dresses looked like sheet-metal, straight up and down. But then if you'd got nothing up here (the description turning graphic), you wouldn't want to call attention to it, would you? And them cheekbones. She looks like a kite; she's all wings—hips, face . . . One of these days you'll be looking up at my undies and see her fly over.

"You need someone with a bit more bounce," she said now, raising her legs again.

"You're bouncy enough for me. Let's get back to this job at the sleaze joint. You can't take that job—"

"Don't be such an old stick, Super. It's a leg up, init?" Her own legs came slowly down.

"Leg up, hell. From King Arthur's to Soho is leaving a cesspool for a sewer."

She puffed with the exertion of lowering her legs back over her head. "All the Q.T. Club wants is that the hostesses see the clientele don't run out of drinks and chips. You know, for the gambling."

"Oh, don't I know. The whole Dirty Squad knows. You look like a pretzel."

She turned her head and stuck out her tongue.

"That wheel's so rigged you could hoist a mainsail on it." Carole-anne sighed and sat up. "You should see the gown I wear—"

"No, thanks."

Her hands were on her hips. "Lord, you're wors'n an old mum." She tossed her head. It was a poor attempt at hauteur with a pile of red-gold curls spilling across her face.

Jury sighed. He could sympathize with the old mums of this world, trying to convince their kids they shouldn't do what they didn't want to do anyway. Well, he supposed the kids had to beat up on someone because they were mad at themselves at not having the nerve to undertake what was usually some harrowing scheme involving danger.

"You have to be twenty-one to work in that place. You're under."

It was worse than telling her she was ugly. "I'm *not* under. I'm over. Twenty-two."

"No kidding? Last week you were twenty-five when you went looking for that steno job. Twenty-five being the age they wanted. Age melts from thy divine countenance."

She changed the subject. "How long you going to be gone?"

"Five minutes. Long enough to put the Q.T. Club out of business."

"God! Leave off!" She picked up a pillow.

Jury felt a soft thud on his forehead. "And what about the theater? You can't work nights and keep your job."

She flounced back on the couch. "It's not even West End. Camden-bloody-Town! You call that *theater?*"

"Just call the club and tell them you regret you must leave town. Say your old mum is dying."

Now she was turned on her side doing quick scissor-cuts with her legs. "Is SB-stroke-H coming over, then?"

"Susan is her name. Yes, for a bit."

Carole-anne sat up again and cut him dead with a look from eyes the color of the Aegean. At least Jury imagined that was what the Aegean must be like, deep shimmering blue blending into the purple horizon. "Tonight we was to go down the Angel." She flopped back, dead.

"I'm really sorry, Carole-anne. I was supposed to see Susan last night and I didn't."

Points for him, having stood up Susan. Carole-anne relented and struck a languid pose, dangling her espadrille on her toes. "You want to go to bed with a frozen lolly, I don't mind."

Jury shut his eyes, not so much to shut out Carole-anne's nattering as to defrost the image of Susan she'd just conjured up. "Who I go to bed with is kind of my business, wouldn't you say?"

No, she wouldn't. She started peeling the new polish from her thumbnail and said, "You gotta be careful of flopping in the sack with just *anyone—*"

"Carole-*anne.*" It was the dangerous tone.

Which bothered Carole-anne no more than the sandal she was fitting on her small white foot, Cinderella-wise. "What time is it?"

Jury was suspicious. Carole-anne never cared about time when she was using his flat, for whatever purpose. He felt as if he were living on the time-share plan. "Half-past five. Why?"

She rose and stretched, a sight not just for the sore-eyed but for the blind. "Oh, just thought I'd go for a walk." Arms straight out, she turned from the waist. "What time's SB-stroke-H coming?" Round to the right, round to the left . . .

As if she didn't know. "Eight. Why?"

Her calisthenics continued. Deep kneebends now. She shrugged at the same time. "Nothing." She ended with a split.

"You can be the house cheerleader. Listen, while I'm gone, keep an eye on Mrs. Wassermann, will you? Take her to the Bingo in Upper Street, or something."

Carole-anne stopped halfway down to the floor. *"Bingo?"*

He might as well have asked her to visit a nunnery. "Sure. She's got chums that go there every week."

"Welllll . . ."

"There's a surprise in it for you."

Carole-anne loved surprises. "Sure, I'll take her to Bingo. Don't I always look out for Mrs. W?"

She did, actually. Jury said, "I've found a job for you."

Still split, she took the card he held out. "That's a *surprise?* What's this?" She looked down at the card.

"You'll love it. You get to wear a costume, Carole-anne."

That got her attention. Carole-anne would have gone down the mines if a costume were part of the job. It was one of the reasons she loved acting and was good at it.

"What sort?" Her eyes glittered as she scooped herself off the floor.

"Oh, one part of it's a sort of satin turban. With stars all over it. You get to tell fortunes." He smiled at her own wide smile. Carole-anne was having a good enough time predicting Jury's future. Imagine turning her loose on perfect strangers, knowledge of whose lives would be uncluttered by reality. She'd be moving the planets about to suit herself. In a walk to the Angel pub she'd tried to convince him that the twinkling light on top of the post office building was Halley's Comet.

"Is it a fair, like? Do I have a booth?"

"It's a shop, actually. I'm not sure about the booth." He handed her the little card. "The proprietor wants you to come round right away. Madame Zostra, that's who you're to be," he added. *"Madame Zostra, famous clairvoyant"* . . . where had he read that?

" 'Starrdust,' fancy that," she said, studying the card. "Whatever do they sell?"

Jury smiled. "Oh, different things. Dreams, maybe."

Carole-anne sighed and shoved the card into the band of her shorts. "If SB-stroke-H is coming, you'll need one, Super."

Her espadrilles slapped out and up the stairs.

Susan Bredon-Hunt, who was walking about the room barefoot, in her silky teddies, was talking about a future she seemed to think was theirs. She talked a great deal, Susan did. Immediately she came into his flat, she would undress, but not, he had found, out of a desire to go straight to bed, or even to appear engagingly wanton. She seemed to need to undress to calculate. Prancing back and forth (there was something equine about Susan, who rode to hounds), she smoked and drank her wine. The bowl of the glass she held cupped in her hands like a little crystal ball in which she read their future.

". . . and it's time you met Daddy, Richard. I just lunched with him today at Claridge's and he wants you to come round for cocktails. . . ."

And so forth. It depressed him to think of it, really. The manor house somewhere in Suffolk. A star-studded family of all sorts of variations of the Most Excellent Order of the British Empire. Here a CBE, there a few OBEs, no lowly MBEs, of course. Daddy, he remembered, was a Knight of the Thistle. Jury imagined that he himself appealed to some sense of recklessness in Susan, the desire to do something shocking like marrying a civil servant, a policeman.

He wished she would stop her pacing and planning and talking about the future they most certainly would never share. Even a fight about the other night when he had left so suddenly would have been a relief, would have made him feel closer to her. But when he had brought it up, she had simply brushed it aside and went on to talk about the future, their future, as if she were dressing a window in some fashionable matchings of escritoires and turkey carpets.

As she paced by his chair, he reached out and pulled her down on his lap, spilling a little of the wine across the peach silk that covered her small breasts. He ran his hands down her sides, from the angles of the shoulders to the bony hips, as she scraped at the wine stain.

"This is brand-new, Richard," she said, pouting.

"I'll buy you another." He buried his face in the curve of her neck—

There was a knock at the door.

He knew who it was.

"Oh, I *hope* I'm not interrupting—" said the tenant from upstairs. Carole-anne Nouveau was wearing a fire-brigade-red dress, down the front of which any man would have loved to dump a cask of wine. The neck was scooped out in a diamond shape, the mandarin collar tightened by some sparkly bit of fake-diamond costume jewelry. The tightness elsewhere didn't need diamonds. He could not believe that she was carrying a casserole, whose steam emitted wonderful vapors. "Your favorite." She smiled sweetly.

He had no idea what his favorite was, but he was suddenly hungry as hell. For drink, food, sex. "Thank you," he said, straight-faced.

"And here's that song . . ." Sweet smile. She sashayed over to the record player, put the casserole down, and took the record from its sleeve. She clicked the button, turned to Jury, and winked, if such a languorous movement of the eyelash could be called a wink. "You remember . . . well . . ."

On an extended sigh she listened to a few bars. *"Of all the girls I LOVED before . . ."* Dreamily, she held Jury's eye long enough for a countdown on a launch pad. "That's Julio. You remember Spain."

The only Spain he'd ever shared with Carole-anne had lasted for twenty minutes in the lobby of the Regency Hotel. He glared at her as Julio remembered the girls he'd loved going in and out his door.

Carole-anne pretended not to notice Jury's black look as she shoved the casserole up against Susan's apricot bosom, and (in a totally different voice) said, "Ten minutes on top of the cooker, dear. Ta."

The steam coming off the casserole could not compete with the steam coming off Susan Bredon-Hunt.

Jury stowed his things in the car next morning and went down the steps to the basement flat. He was surprised to find the door slightly ajar and the heavy drapes open. Mrs. Wassermann had enough deadbolts for a locksmith's display case, and it usually took five minutes just for her to open the door. Not today, though. Since Carole-anne had taken the upstairs flat a year ago, Mrs. Wassermann had lowered the drawbridge of her fortress flat and let in a little light.

"I just dropped in to see if you'd like something from Brighton," Jury said when she came in from the kitchen. Over her navy blue dress she was wearing an apron. Her hair was pulled back from her face and wound in a coil as neat and tight as a clockspring.

"Ah! Mr. Jury, I'm glad you're having a little holiday. Just wait, there is something I have for you."

"Not a holiday, Mrs. Wassermann," he called after her. "I only wish it were."

While he waited, he looked around the flat; with the sun warming the windowpanes and tossing coins of light on the brightly patterned rug she'd brought from Poland, it looked much different from the dark room with the drawn drapes and armored door. But Jury could understand her fears; Mrs. Wassermann had reached her sixties by various escape routes—back alleys, tunnels, blockaded roads, barbed-wire fences. That was when she was young, in what she always called the Big War. It was something they shared, despite the difference in their ages—the loss of her family, the loss of his.

She came in carrying a small parcel tied up with string. "For your trip, I made this. Sandwiches. Breast of turkey, the very best, and a cheese and pickle."

He thanked her and took the parcel. "Keep an eye on Carole-anne, will you? Maybe you could have her down for tea. Maybe you could take her to your Bingo night. She might not show it, but I think she gets lonely."

"Such a sweet child, Mr. Jury." They were walking up the three steps to the pavement. "Isn't it nice about her new job?"

Jury was suspicious. He didn't think Carole-anne could have told Mrs. Wassermann yet about Starrdust. And God knows she would never have mentioned the job she'd meant to take at the Q.T. Club. "New job?"

"You know, in the all-night launderette. Carole-anne said she was to work the late shift and wouldn't be home until the wee hours. Well, I told her she must be careful and to take a taxi."

"The launderette. Yes, I'd forgotten about that."

"So much better than her old job."

The old job was at King Arthur's as a topless dancer. "Yes, much better."

"At the library."

Jury studied the pavement at his feet, then looked up when the front door opened and the Librarian came out in her skintight jeans and fake-fur jacket. "Much as she likes books, it just didn't pay enough, I expect."

"Ah, so hard it is to find work these days. And at the launderette she gets to wash her clothes free."

"Hi, Mrs. W!" Carole-anne called gaily.

"Hello, dear," said Mrs. Wassermann. "Don't you look lovely!"

"Thanks, Mrs. W. On my way to see about a job." She was looking everywhere but at Jury, up and down the street, at the sky, checking for snow, rain, sun—anything but Jury's expression.

"Hello, dear," said Jury with a mock-sweetness he seldom indulged in. "When you get through with the turban and stars, you can do my laundry."

Carole-anne squinted up at him, slack-mouthed, as if she weren't sure about this unclean stranger on their doorstep. Her creamy forehead puckered; her raindrop earrings stirred. "Huh? Well, I gotta go. Ta." She blew a kiss and hitched her bag over her shoulder.

They watched her go down the street. First one, then another of the male residents coming the other way did an about-face when she passed. Across the way, a small man in a bowler latched his gate and did a quick-step, following up the other two. The postman moved a little more spryly about his duties, stuffing letters any old way through the slots of doors along Carole-anne's route.

"Well, Mrs. Wassermann, there goes the neighborhood," said Jury, with a smile.

PART V

The Old Penny Palace

22

"**B**RIGHTON is known for the brilliancy of its air," said Jury, looking out over the gunmetal water toward a horizon lost in fog.

Eyes squinted nearly shut in case of sea-spray, Wiggins gave his long scarf one more turn around his neck and looked as if he couldn't care a pence for brilliancy.

Jury flicked away his cigarette and took a deep breath.

"It's not healthy, sir."

"Breathing?"

"The sea air," said Wiggins, adding instructively, "no matter what people say, any doctor can tell you it's not healthy." He then brought out his Fisherman's Friends, a staple in his portable pharmacy ever since the cold, damp days of Dorset. He pushed the packet at Jury. "These'll help a bad throat."

"I haven't got one, Wiggins."

"You will," said the sergeant almost merrily. He put one in Jury's hand.

Wiggins, thought Jury, would have taken shock treatments to ward off flu. "Mind over matter" was not a phrase in the Wiggins lexicon. "There's Paul Swann, or I think it must be." Jury pointed over the railing, down the shingle beach. "Near the Palace Pier."

The char had told Jury that Mr. Swann was not in, that he'd gone down to the beach, to the Palace Pier. Yesterday, it'd been the Royal Pavilion, she said. "Did the East portico. Last week he did the main entrance. He's doing it all, see, inside too," she added, as if Swann did floors.

Paul Swann sat on a canvas stool, looking far down the strand toward the West Pier. Sketchbook and paints sat at his feet, a watercolor rested on the easel before him. He was a man of indeterminate age with a thin face and watery blue eyes.

After Jury introduced himself, Swann suggested they sit on a nearby bench within sight of his painting. An interview in the open air, brilliant though it might be, only made Wiggins cough.

Paul Swann said sympathetically, "Not sick are you, Mr. Wiggins?"

"Not yet, thank you." Wiggins shrugged down into his topcoat.

As they sat down on the bench, Swann said, in answer to Jury's question about David Marr, "I don't really see David that often, so I'm afraid I can't be of much help to you there, Superintendent. Very nice chap, though," he said hurriedly and intently, as if he were concerned that his lack of intimacy with Marr might be construed as his handing him over to police.

"You were in the Running Footman that night, Mr. Swann, weren't you?"

"That's right, I was. Been thinking about it too, trying to remember exactly when he left, what Ivy did, those details." He shook his head. "But I wasn't absolutely sober and I wasn't really paying attention. I think she collected her coat and left just as time was called."

"She said nothing to you?"

"No, nothing."

Wiggins came up out of his shivery cocoon long enough to ask, "How well did you know this Ivy Childess, Mr. Swann?" Turtle-wise, his neck drew back inside his scarf to receive the answer.

"There was a drinks party at the house in Knightsbridge. I went round with David, who had the Childess girl in tow." He stopped and looked up at the sky. "Would you just pardon me a moment." Swann walked across the shingle to collect his easel and palette. "Hope you don't mind. There's just a touch to put to this before the light fades." He continued his assessment of Ivy Childess. "What on earth David saw in that little chit is beyond me. I know that he is not a stupid man, nor a lascivious one—oh, Ivy was quite plump and juicy—and that all of his wild drinking and so forth is merely flinging grit in the eyes." As if flicking a bit of that grit away, he touched the brush, dipped in pale, pale yellow, to the picture of the West Pier.

"Why would he want to fling it, Mr. Swann?"

"I don't know. We all have things to hide, Superintendent. Including the sort of person we really are."

Jury smiled. "Difficult to do with you. I've seen your portraits of the Winslows."

Swann looked up from his painting, smiling. "I'd say that's quite a compliment. Well, I am very good at portraiture, but I will only paint certain people. I'd be a rich man if I took on every commission I was offered; I turn most of them down. I find most people much too shallow or simpering or narcissistic to want to bother with."

"But not the Winslows?"

He smiled. "No, most definitely not the Winslows." Arms folded across his chest, he kept his eye on his watercolor, so intently that he might have been expecting the pier to move, the fog to shift. "That was the only time I'd seen Hugh Winslow, at that party in Knightsbridge. He's the wild card, isn't he?"

Jury looked at him. "Wild card?"

"Doesn't carry the Winslow stamp. I wanted Hugh in that portrait; I thought it would round it out. But when I met him, or when I watched him with the others—especially Marion and Edward—I realized it wouldn't have done. There's this interesting chemistry amongst them, Mr. Jury. Perhaps you've noticed—?"

"Definitely."

Swann, almost as if he were reworking the Winslow portrait, leaned forward, and applied a faint wash of the pale yellow. "That's it, I think. Anyway, when the three of them are together, they become more than the sum of their parts. They *are* a painting, Mr. Jury. They absolutely *are*. I'm sorry I can't help you out in a more practical way—time David went to the Running Footman, time he returned, et cetera, but I just don't know. As for Ivy Childess, it was only on that one evening, and not much of that. I only stayed for half an hour or so. Hate cocktail parties. Much rather go down to the Shepherd Tavern for drinks. I do hope it's not going to go badly for David; I honestly can't see him killing that girl." He shrugged and looked truly sad that he couldn't help out either Jury or David Marr.

"There's another painting there, Mr. Swann, a portrait you probably did?"

"Yes, Rose and Phoebe. Rose Winslow walked out on Edward. You can imagine," he added shaking his head.

It was as though any such behavior on the part of one of them would cause the others to close ranks completely. Jury thought of Hugh Winslow. "Did you hear any talk of another man, someone who perhaps, well, lured Rose Winslow away?"

Paul Swann stared at him, and then he laughed. "Lure *Rose?* Good God, I should certainly think it would be the other way round. Poor Ned."

"Did David Marr ever mention her?"

"Yes. He disliked her. Well, she wasn't very likable, you see."

His voice slightly muffled, Wiggins said, "Seems strange they'd keep her picture about, in the circumstances."

"It's because of Phoebe," said Swann. "It's really all they've got left of Phoebe."

Jury looked at the watercolor, the strange milky light of the fog he'd captured that blanketed the pier. "Did you ever hear Marr mention a woman named Sheila Broome at all?"

"Broome? No, never."

"Well, it was just a long shot, Mr. Swann. Thanks."

Wiggins had been studying the watercolor and said, "You know, that's good. That yellow you just put on. Changes the whole thing, really. Makes it look like it's floating."

"Ah, that's just it, Mr. Wiggins. Thank you. You've a grand eye. Do you dabble in the paint pots too?"

"Just a bit," said Wiggins, without a pause. "Sunday painter, that sort of thing."

Jury looked out to sea. Whenever Wiggins found himself in the presence of art, literature, music, a new persona evolved out of the fog, a form taking shape right before Jury's eyes. At any rate, with Swann's speaking to him like a brother, Wiggins had begun to unwind the labyrinthine scarf.

And to include Paul Swann in the elite group of those Wiggins would like to save from certain death. "Care for one, Mr. Swann?"

Paul Swann thanked him and held up the amber lozenge in the fading light. "That is a truly remarkable color."

"I've always thought so, Mr. Swann," he said innocently, holding up its mate in the same way.

Jury scuffed at the broken shells at his feet and was rather sorry his own inartistic eye could identify nothing much but tan beach and gray water. The conversation had switched to literature.

"Sometimes I wonder if Coleridge's dream about Kubla Khan was inspired by George the Fourth and his plans for the Pavilion. The renovation had been going on for ten years when he wrote 'Kubla Khan.' " Paul Swann smiled. " 'His flashing eyes, his floating hair.' Can you think of a better candidate for him than the Prince Regent who 'fed on honeydew and drank the milk of paradise'?"

"I never thought of it exactly that way," said Wiggins.

Jury shook his head. If he ever thought of it any way, it was news to Jury.

"And Mrs. Fitzherbert, the only woman he ever loved, according to George, might have also been the perfect candidate for the poor woman 'wailing for her demon-lover.' " Paul Swann sighed and gathered up his paints and sketches and brushes. "Love, love, hmm. I suppose I don't truly qualify as an artist, never having known the turbulence of heartrending passion. But to tell the truth, seeing all the misery it causes, I just thought I'd give it a miss." He grinned. "I imagine the *crime passionnel* keeps you in work. Do you think this is one, this case?"

Jury said, sadly, "There's certainly enough passion to go round, Mr. Swann."

Swann left them and they walked down the Promenade, past the pub, what looked like changing rooms, a video place where chairs and tables were set up outside for people wanting coffee and soft drinks.

Next door, a fellow was busy slapping paint on the facade of a little museum of antique slot machines, called the Old Penny Palace. He laid down his brush and went inside. Wiggins studied the poster describing some of the machines on display and said, "Look at this, will you?" He pointed to a strength-tester. "Haven't seen one of those since I was a kid. Good for the circulation." He raised his arm, tried to make a muscle. "And over there. Tell your fortune, that does. One of those booths where you pick up a phone and a voice tells you your future."

"A voice from the next world, Wiggins?"

"I know it's just a tape that runs over and over. Still, I wouldn't mind giving it a try. Could we stop here for a minute, do you think?"

While Wiggins talked to the young fellow behind the counter, Jury waited beside the Laughing Sailor. It was dressed in a navy blue uniform and sported a white cap over its sad painted eyes.

"He said the place wasn't open yet, he's trying to get it ready for its opening," said Wiggins.

"Then how'd you get these?" Jury held up a token.

Wiggins counted his tokens, frowning. "Well, I just happened to show him my warrant—"

"Wiggins!"

"No harm done, no harm, sir. Try a few machines; it'll take your mind off things."

"I'm going next door for a cup of coffee." He was looking at the poster near the door listing some of the museum's offerings. "I wonder what the butler saw."

He sat with his Styrofoam cup and a foil-wrapped packet of peanuts. He pushed the peanuts in a circle, assigning to the spokes of this wheel the different signs—Aries, Gemini, Sagittarius. Jury looked at the peanut planets and wondered ruefully if perhaps he should take Andrew Starr up on his offer to draw a horoscope, that in it he might find one or two elusive answers.

Disgusted with himself, he dropped the peanuts into a metal ashtray. Murder wasn't in the stars; it was on the ground, his ground. And it would help, he supposed, if any of the people he'd talked with had been his idea of a proper villain. The thin, plain fabric that had been woven around

David Marr and Ivy Childess had now been interwoven with more exotic threads, perhaps obscuring rather than heightening the pattern in the carpet. There was also the disquieting knowledge that Macalvie was right, that solving the murder of Ivy Childess depended upon solving the murder of Sheila Broome.

He stared out at the darkness gathering over the Atlantic and thought about Sheila Broome. Perhaps it was the geography that was throwing him off—connecting her with Exeter when she had, after all, spent a good deal of her time in London. She'd been good-looking, the type Hugh Winslow went for. And if she had threatened, like Ivy Childess, to tell Marion Winslow . . .

Jury rested his head in his hands. Ivy Childess, Hugh Winslow had said, could ferret out anyone's secrets. Jury thought of that bulletin board in David's living room. What if she had ferreted out David Marr's? What had Macalvie said about something worse than murder? *Betrayal of friends and benefactors.*

He felt he needed something, like background music, to silence one part of his mind so that the other could function. Jury drank off his cold coffee without tasting it, started back to the Old Penny Palace.

Through the gathering dusk, he looked down the strand toward the West Pier, floating in the mist.

Then glided in Porphyria . . .

23

⚜

WHEN Dolly had said this morning that she was thinking of moving back to Brighton, Kate had been astonished.
She was tired of London, she said simply, as if that were reason enough for leaving it, though it meant giving up the decorator flat and the job that she'd clawed her way up to. Kate told her she couldn't understand how Dolly could give up what she'd worked so hard to get.

Maybe you don't want me in the house.

Kate didn't immediately say yes, not because she hadn't wanted Dolly here, but because she was too filled with surprise that her sister, who had for years spoken of Brighton as provincial and dull, would even consider living in it.

When she said it again, that Kate must not want her in the house, the tone was so sad that Kate had to put her hand on her sister's arm and give her a little shake. That wasn't true; of course she did, she told Dolly.

Dolly said they'd have plenty of money, more than enough, even without Dolly's high-paying job, and that Kate could stop all of this. "All of this" meaning her taking in boarders. Dolly made a graceful gesture with her arm (wasn't her every move graceful?) taking in the long drawing room where they'd been having a sandwich for lunch.

But she was used to it, Kate said; she didn't really want to give up her little business.

Dolly had shaken and shaken her head, no. It was degrading, running a bed-and-breakfast.

It wasn't for Kate, though. . . .

The reply had been explosive. Then it's *dangerous*. Dolly's hand was shaking and she brought the silver pot down on the table with a thud.

Dangerous? Surely Dolly couldn't be talking about their prospective roomer. Kate tried to laugh, but it stuck in her throat.

Dolly hadn't stayed to answer. Her Cossack hat was already on, and her boots. She walked hurriedly to the door, where she took up her coat and walked out, the door slamming behind her.

All Kate could do was to gather up the cutlery on the tray. That she might be about to harbor an escaped convict, a criminal, made her want to laugh out loud. Yet Dolly's behavior during this visit had been strange, very unlike her, as if she were stuck in the past, talking of things they used to do when they were children. Dolly would stay out for hours and hours when before she'd spent most of the day in her robe, smoking at the breakfast table. Now she would come back with a report of this place and that—the museum, the Pavilion—all places where their father had taken her, dressed in one of those pastel gossamer dresses sprigged with tiny flowers. . . . Perhaps it was his death. Was he reaching out from the grave to make certain she was still his little girl?

Kate could still see Dolly standing before the window the night their father had died, staring out through the dusk, and the rain blown by wind, great long curtains of it, blowing against the window in waves.

24

WIGGINS was trying his luck on the Love-Test. Its lightbulb display did not seem to be making Wiggins happy; the bulb beside "Amorous" was not lighting up. Jury passed the strength-tester and *What the Butler Saw* and stood looking at the machine called *Midnight in the Haunted Graveyard*.

He put in his token and watched the tiny white figures pop up. A skeleton slid out of an opening grave, a dot of white—a ghost—raised itself behind a headstone; another ghost peered from a hole. A cloaked figure fluttered about in this miniature colony of the dead before it disappeared into the wood. Jury's thoughts scattered as the ground reclaimed its skeletons, the stones and trees their apparitions. *Flash cars and flash men. . . . They all loved Phoebe so much. . . . It all fell apart. . . . "Where have you gone to, Elizabeth Vere?"*

"Just a moment, sir," said Wiggins, his eyes glued to the viewer of *What the Butler Saw.*

Jury slammed his hand over the viewer. "You'll have to skip the naughty bits, Wiggins." He wrote in his notebook, tore off the page, and handed it to Wiggins.

"Check to see if Plant called headquarters about the snapshot he took to Exeter—"

"But we've already—"

"I *know* we've already. And find Miles Wells."

Wiggins frowned. "The driver of the car that hit Phoebe Winslow? And ask him exactly what?"

"If the lady in the car was Sheila Broome. And why he drove for several blocks and then came back."

"No one mentioned a lady in the car, sir."

"I just did, Wiggins."

～⌇～⌇～

"Sheila Broome?" said Macalvie, dragging his feet off the desk in the Brighton police station. "But what the hell? Even if it was revenge, why not go for the driver?"

"That's the point. I think she *was* the driver. She'd been arrested once for drunk-driving, Macalvie. If he hadn't taken the rap for her, she'd have been in jail. But to do that, they had to switch seats. Stop the car and switch. I doubt he was simply being a gentleman about it; I imagine he thought it was his neck, too. Better to be booked for an unavoidable accident than for letting your drunk companion drive without a license and run somebody down. The question I asked myself was why little Phoebe ran out into the street."

"So what'd you answer yourself?"

"Hugh Winslow answered. She was angry and frightened; what frightened her was seeing Daddy in bed with a woman who certainly wasn't Mummy—Ivy Childess."

Macalvie looked long and hard at the tips of his run-down shoes, which he'd just planted on the desktop again. Then he said, "So anyone in that family would hold not just Hugh responsible but Ivy. They'd ice her, any one of them, right? Just like Sheila Broome."

"Absolutely. In a way, I suppose, it ricochets: they wouldn't kill him— after all, he's family—they'd kill her."

"Could even have been Hugh himself."

"Yes."

"You're not suggesting it's murder on the Brighton Express, or something? That they were all in on it?"

"No. Only one of them. And I don't think that's the whole of the motive, either." Jury studied the photograph of the Queen hanging on the dull, ocher-colored wall. "I think the motive might be very confused; it has not to do just with the death of Phoebe, but with Rose Winslow. 'Betrayal of friends and benefactors,' that's what you said."

Macalvie sighed. "I wish I'd known what I meant."

Jury sat back, dug his hands in his pockets. "You haven't seen the Winslows; you didn't see what sort of family they are. They're as bonded together as the figures in a portrait. It's unconscious, I think. I doubt the Winslows know what form their punishment takes. Hugh wasn't sent packing, after all. They just stopped communicating. They don't cut you *down,* they cut you *out.* To betray one is to betray all. And David Marr certainly knew that."

"Marr?"

"I'm sure he was having an affair with Rose Winslow. Rose strikes me as being a slightly up-market version of Ivy Childess: selfish, untrustworthy, avaricious. But with enough of a flame-to-moth quality that she singed more than one pair of wings. David Marr's, for example. He's got a collection of stuff in his room—photos, cards. One's from Vegas. He's never been to the States, and according to more than one person, Rose always wanted to go. None of the Winslows, no one, has heard a word from her. So why should David Marr have done, and why keep it a secret?"

"It wouldn't go down a treat with the family. And Ivy Childess found out. Well, well, now Marr has no alibi and a great motive," said Macalvie.

"A touch of blackmail—oh, not for the up-front money. Ivy didn't want to stretch out her days dusting off the stars at the Starrdust. She wanted marriage. Marriage to *any* of the Winslow-Marr family. She'd drop David to pick up Hugh; drop Hugh to pick up David; I'm sure she must have had a bit of a go at Ned, too."

"You're talking jealousy."

Jury raised his eyebrows. "Among *them?* Oh, no. If David had won Ned's girl in a fair fight, or Hugh won David's—the other would have been a gentleman, would have backed out. It's not jealousy; it's betrayal. Betrayal is probably *the* mortal sin with the Winslows." Jury pocketed his cigarettes and said, "Plant's gone to Exeter. He wanted the waitress at the Little Chef to take a look at a photo."

"She's already looked. Something new?"

Macalvie didn't seem surprised. When the wheel stopped, he'd just spin it again.

Jury smiled. "You were right about the connection between those murders, Macalvie."

"That's a relief; for a while, life had lost its music."

"Why in the hell would the killer wait so long? Phoebe Winslow died nearly a year before Sheila Broome."

"So there wouldn't appear to be a connection. But that's just the opinion of your standard, plodding detective."

"If there's anything you aren't, it's 'standard.' " And then it occurred to Jury that he hadn't known Macalvie was even *in* Brighton. But it didn't surprise Jury that he was. The standard, plodding detective would follow a tidal wave if a clue were tossing about on its crest. "Why're you here, Macalvie?"

A police constable stuck his face around the door to tell Jury someone had called about an hour before and left him a message, which he handed to Jury. "He said his name was Plant, sir. Mr. Melrose Plant. That he was leaving Exeter, but that he'd get in touch later. I was careful to write it down, sir, since it was a bit odd." The constable frowned with the oddity of it and ducked out.

"*Weren't they* all *Porphyria?*" Jury read the note to Macalvie, who sighed and said, "Does he have to send his messages in code?"

"Well, obviously he means they were all alike—they were, too: that long, blond hair. Selfish, avaricious." Jury frowned, remembering the photos in the drawing room of the Winslows' house. "And so far as the hair goes . . . even Phoebe Winslow."

Macalvie was drawing a newspaper clipping from his wallet. "My little bit of news comes straight from chocolate flake country." He unfolded the strip of paper and handed it to Jury. "We'd better get the lead out, Jury. There's someone wandering around Brighton who's in considerable danger."

"Who?"

Macalvie turned the newspaper around so that it faced Jury. It was a cutout from the entertainment section. "The Rainlady."

Jury looked at the pretty girl in the picture, at the heart-shaped face and long, blond hair. "You found her. Jimmy Rees finally told you?"

"Hell, no. He's still back there with chocolate flake coming out of his ears. It was the telly, Jury. I was in your office and flicked on Wiggins's set to catch the news. I thought maybe some Fleet Street reporter could tell me who killed Sheila and Ivy. Anyway, the ten-twenty news is supposed to end with this pretty lady coming out in a white slicker and umbrella. It's always raining, see, at ten-twenty. She's the weather girl. Her name is Dolly Sands and she took it with her, in a manner of speaking. Very suddenly she felt she needed a holiday. Dolly Sands lives here in Brighton." Macalvie was shrugging into his coat. "And I think we better find her before she takes a permanent holiday."

25

THE woman who came to the door was tall and attractive, with taffy-colored hair that fell smoothly from a center part to her chin. Once the hair might have been as light as that of the girl in the newspaper clipping. Her blouse was mustard-colored, good silk, but flattering neither in shade nor in fit. She had the diffident air of one who doesn't know how good-looking she is, or hasn't been told it often enough. Most of life no doubt lived in the shadow of her beautiful sister.

"Kate Sandys?" asked Jury, showing her his warrant card. As if uncertain whether to admit to her name, silently she looked from Jury to Macalvie and back to the warrant card. "We need to talk to your sister, Miss Sandys. Is she here?"

"Dolly? No. No, she isn't here. What do you want?" She looked over her shoulder at the hall behind her. It was as if the house belonged to someone else.

Macalvie was standing to Jury's left, leaning against the doorjamb. "To come in, for starters." He put his hand flat against the door and shoved it back.

Her eyes widened. "Why? What's happened? Has something happened to Dolly?"

"We don't know yet."

Nervously, she gestured for them to come in. She pushed one sleeve of her silk blouse up, ran a hand over the light brown hair, silky as the blouse. Macalvie brushed by her, stood in the hallway looking round, his hands shoved in his pockets as if he were observing the scene of a crime.

Kate Sandys led them into a large, chilly drawing room. Jury noticed a photograph album lying open on a library table, a coat and scarf across the arm of a sofa, a letter on the mantel above the unlit fireplace. Over the years, Jury had grown more and more aware of the way in which some houses, some rooms seemed to bear witness to the end of something—a death, an imminent departure. Perhaps it was the closeness to the sea here that intensified that image. The sea, the photographs of old Brighton on the wall, the watercolor of the deck of an ocean liner, dim figures by the rail waving, an attempt to be gay and lighthearted amidst the flutter of colored streamers. He glanced around him, almost expecting to see the furniture sheeted, the steamer trunk packed, the cab at the door in the fog.

In answer to a question from Macalvie, Kate said, "She's gone out."

"Out where?"

"I don't know."

"Think."

She didn't answer; instead she kept her gaze fixed on Jury's face, as if it were the more hospitable of the two. "You still haven't told me why you want her, or what's happened."

"Your sister Dolly may be in big trouble, a lot of danger," said Macalvie.

"*What* danger?" Her hand went to her neck, fingers worrying the thin gold chain on her breast.

Jury told her about the Hays Mews murder. "We think your sister might have seen something, might have seen the killer even—"

Kate sat down suddenly. "You mean he's come *here*, to Brighton? But how would he know who—?"

"Easy," said Macalvie. "Dolly Sandys walks right into his living room every weekday night. Three days ago she calls in sick to the studio, packs a bag, and comes here. It was your name and address they had in case of emergency. And we weren't the only ones that had come inquiring after her. So you'd better think very hard."

"That's why she's been so moody; ever since she came I've been wondering why and what's wrong with her."

"Have you seen anyone hanging about, Miss Sandys? Any strangers?"

She looked up anxiously. "No. Well, yes, in a way. There was a man in the Spotted Dog, that's a pub not far from here. We got to chatting; he mentioned he was looking for a room. . . ." She spread her hands. "I told him about our house." Her voice was strained. "Later, when I thought about it, I wondered if he was the man I'd seen earlier, when I went to the Pavilion. When I came out and started walking across Castle Square, I saw him standing down at the end of the walk. It was unnerving; he seemed to be watching me. As if he was following me."

"What'd your sister say when you told her?"

"But I didn't, you see. Dolly left the house early in the afternoon to go to Pia Negra's. She's a fortune-teller, a clairvoyant with a place in the Lanes. I know she came back because she changed coats—she left the fur and took the rain slicker. But I haven't seen her."

"You say she went to this fortune-teller. Exactly where in the Lanes?"

"Black Horse Lane."

Macalvie wrote it down. "Okay, where else could she have gone? Favorite pub? Shop? Restaurant?"

Kate shook her head.

"You better think it up, Miss Sandys. Your sister's out there with a killer."

She flinched as if he'd slapped her. "I'm trying to think." She rolled the gold necklace between the palms of her hands. "I thought it was a man, that she was having trouble over a man."

"She is. Big trouble."

26

HE watched her as she stood in the weak arc of light coming from the entryway to the Old Penny Palace. She was standing there, pulling the collar of the bright, white slicker round her throat, considering. Her face was pale, filtered through the drizzling rain that had started a few minutes ago. Perhaps she was looking for shelter. She went in.

Except for the pub farther down, everything else was shut up tightly along this causeway of amusement arcades underneath the arches of the King's Road, between the two piers. There was no one about. From the direction of the West Pier came the barking of a dog, excited perhaps because of its proximity to the water. But he saw no one, nothing. The only illumination came from the sodium lamps above, along the King's Road; that, and the sickly yellow light shining out from the Penny Palace.

Except for her, the museum looked empty. Someone must have been spiffing it up, for there was a bucket of marine blue paint on the counter with a brush across its top. The owner or whoever was doing the painting was gone, perhaps gone along to the pub under the arches for a drink. There was no one but the two of them, nothing but the wooden figure called the Laughing Sailor inside his wood-and-glass cage, there beside the entrance to greet the customers if they had a penny to make him laugh.

When she had left the house on Madeira Drive, he'd followed, as he'd followed her twice before. Those times, though, it had been daylight, and she'd led him in the other direction, away from the seawall toward the center of the town and the brick-paved alleys of the Lanes, a maze of narrow streets like a spiderweb.

It had been difficult watching the house; there were no newsagents, no shops or restaurants he might have gone into, as there'd been in Exeter. So he had watched from several different vantage points from King's Road and the seawall, leaning against a railing, pretending to read a newspaper or to look out over the sea. And the surveillance—at which he felt he was no good at all—had to be interrupted by going off for a meal, or to the toilet, then coming back, then going off again.

He had considered going up to the house when the other one had gone out. The sister. They looked enough alike to be sisters. Older, a little taller, but without that strangely compelling presence that made the younger one so popular. How odd that he should recognize a television personality; that news broadcast with its trendy little weather report was the only thing he watched. Otherwise, he would never have found her. And whether it was her face or whether that white slicker she always wore, he didn't know. As he followed her, he watched men turn as they passed her, turn and stare.

He moved closer. There was a counter for making change, dispensing the big pennies that were necessary to work the machines. He watched her moving about through the thicket of machines, stopping to look at the crane in its fancy glass enclosure. She must have had some of the pennies with her from an earlier visit or perhaps she'd nicked a few from the counter, for she reached in her pocket and in a moment he saw the crane move. After a moment she moved away, circled some more of the machines, sometimes cupping her hands around her face and peering through glass. Against the far wall was a player piano; she studied it for a moment, slugged a coin into it, and soon the tinny, broken sounds of music filled the night.

He stepped back into the shadows of the awning of the place next door that housed video games and a coffee bar when he saw someone coming along the Parade, hurrying now. Probably the owner or whoever had left the machines untended. He could hear voices, brief laughter. It would be difficult to be angry with her; she was too pretty. And probably whoever was in there was bored, maybe lonely.

He listened to the rattling, broken-sounding notes from the piano, remembered the words: ". . . *trade it for a basket of sunshine and flowers.*"

"Pennies from Heaven," it was called. Where had the sunshine gone, and the flowers? He looked up at the night sky, black as lacquer, studded with stars, and thought how much it was like that other night long ago. Darkness, stars, music . . .

He heard her say good-bye. On the way out she—or perhaps the painter —must have dropped a coin into the wooden sailor. There was a short, guttural, donkeylike laugh that stopped suddenly when the music stopped.

And in a few moments, she came out. Stood, looking up at the black sky, as if calculating how long it would be before the rain got heavy, turned up the collar of her white raincoat, and walked on into the darkness toward the steps that led up to the King's Road.

He passed the Laughing Sailor, its wooden jaw locked, mouth hinged in a permanent grin.

Kate Sandys was weeping; Jury knew she couldn't help it, that she was frantic with trying to think of the first place Dolly might have gone to. Macalvie had convinced her that there might not be time to find a second.

She dried her eyes and looked down at the small photo of David Marr. It was a horror; she had actually been going to let him a room.

"It'll be all right, Kate." He leaned toward her, took her hand. "Try to relax."

"I've always been—envious of her, always said she was spoiled. I don't know now. I know I should have taken her more seriously."

"Great," said Macalvie, who was still standing. "That's great but it's not finding her." He snapped shut the photograph album he'd been looking at. "The Brighton police will have gone to everyplace you've mentioned by now—but that doesn't mean she'll be at one of them." He held up the album, frowning. "You leave this here?"

Kate wiped her eyes and looked up. "No. Dolly must've."

"She was going through her childhood pictures, mostly of the pier and the sweet stands and stuff along the oceanfront. Does she go in for it still?"

"The King's Road Arches arcade. Dolly loved the arcade more than anyplace."

"Let's go, Jury." Macalvie started for the door.

Jury put the album in Kate Sandys's lap, wondering why he thought that would be any comfort. Yet, she wrapped her fingers round it as if the memories were real, staring straight ahead.

Then he picked up and pocketed the picture of David Marr. He shook his head. David hadn't been there, he hadn't seen it. And he thought Plant was right about their all having run together, in the mind of the murderer, as the faithless Porphyria. He looked again at the photo he'd been holding of David Marr. But it wasn't the first time, he supposed, he'd been wrong. And God knows, it wouldn't be the last.

She didn't walk up the steps to the King's Road after all; instead, she left the paved walk for the shingle beach. She stopped for a moment to look out to sea, shading her face with her hand, as if it were broad daylight and one could actually see out there, as if she were looking for the bright, bobbing head of a bather. She picked a pebble from the shingle and threw it and continued down the strand, the white raincoat dazzling in the night, a long, yellow scarf fluttering behind her.

He had carried a gun before and he carried it now. At this time of year, though, a woman could be depended on to wear a scarf, and she wore hers as the others had done, ends dangling down the back.

She was walking slowly enough that his catching her up might seem natural to her. Apparently it did, for when he spoke, she merely turned and looked at him, brushing back her hair with her hand.

He told her he was sorry if he seemed to be following her, that she looked so much like someone he used to know.

And did he look familiar to her? he wondered. He could not believe that his face was not engraved on her mind, etched on her eyes the way the victim is said to carry the image of the murderer.

Yet she looked at him almost sightlessly and for some moments. There was a strange expression in her blue eyes, a look of acceptance—he might even have said of complicity. The scarf was unwound, removed. It too was white, and it trailed from her coat pocket. It wasn't a yellow scarf fluttering behind her, but her hair. How could he have mistaken one for the other?

She said that a lot of people took her for someone else; she said she looked like the woman on the telly who did the weather report.

There was nothing in her manner to suggest she recognized him; her voice was flat, expressionless.

Did she live in Brighton? Did she like it?

All of her life, she said; lately she'd been living in London, but she thought she would move back. Then she looked out to sea, said she remembered it the way it was when she was young.

When she was young. Of course, she must have meant when she was a child, but it was still an odd thing to say, as if youth were lost to her, had receded like the wrinkled waves drawing back from the shore.

Looking up at him, she said, *Dolly Sands.* That's who she reminded people of.

Rose, he said. That's who you remind me of. She did not seem to think it was odd that he had said *Rose.*

Then he was silent. That was wrong, somehow. Phoebe, it was Phoebe he was thinking about, wasn't it? Phoebe with all of her flaxen hair spread out in the street.

His hand reached toward her hair; she drew back. As he turned his head, he saw the lights of cars, blue domes whirring up there along the King's Road. A voice hailed him and was carried off by the wind.

Someone screamed. And then she broke from his arms and started to run. There was shouting, torches burning and circling like little moons, people scrambling down the steps.

Before he raised the gun he had time to think of the irony of this. That he hadn't meant to hurt her; she hadn't even known who he was.

The voice that had hailed him called out again: *"Ned!"*

He felt the gun heavy in his hand. Strange that he hadn't felt angry with David. But he shouldn't have told him he was coming here; he should have known David would follow him.

Ned heard the explosion, felt nothing, saw a terrible white glare—stars showering like meteors, moon breaking like a mirror, raincoat flying down the strand.